Waiting for
Ricky Tantrum

Waiting for
Ricky Tantrum

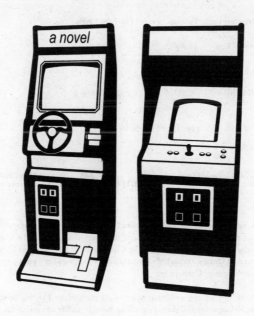

a novel

JULES LEWIS

DUNDURN PRESS
TORONTO

Editor: Michael Carroll
Design: Jennifer Scott
Printer: Webcom

Library and Archives Canada Cataloguing in Publication

Lewis, Jules
      Waiting for Ricky Tantrum : a novel / by Jules Lewis.

ISBN 978-1-55488-740-8

I. Title.

PS8623.E9655W35 2010   C813'.6   C2009-907534-2

1 2 3 4 5   14 13 12 11 10

Conseil des Arts du Canada   Canada Council for the Arts   Canada   ONTARIO ARTS COUNCIL CONSEIL DES ARTS DE L'ONTARIO

We acknowledge the support of the Canada Council for the Arts and the Ontario Arts Council for our publishing program. We also acknowledge the financial support of the Government of Canada through the Canada Book Fund and The Association for the Export of Canadian Books, and the Government of Ontario through the Ontario Book Publishers Tax Credit program, and the Ontario Media Development Corporation.

Care has been taken to trace the ownership of copyright material used in this book. The author and the publisher welcome any information enabling them to rectify any references or credits in subsequent editions.

J. Kirk Howard, President

Printed and bound in Canada.
www.dundurn.com

Dundurn Press
3 Church Street, Suite 500
Toronto, Ontario, Canada
M5E 1M2

Gazelle Book Services Limited
White Cross Mills
High Town, Lancaster, England
LA1 4XS

Dundurn Press
2250 Military Road
Tonawanda, NY
U.S.A. 14150

Mixed Sources
Product group from well-managed forests, controlled sources and recycled wood or fiber
www.fsc.org Cert no. SW-COC-002358
© 1996 Forest Stewardship Council
FSC

ANCIENT FOREST ™
FRIENDLY

for my parents

Relling: All the world is sick, pretty nearly — that's the worst of it.

Gregers: And what treatment are you using for Hjalmar?

Relling: My usual one. I am trying to keep the make-believe of life in him.

Gregers: The make-believe? I don't think I heard you aright.

Relling: Yes, I said make-believe. That is the stimulating principle of life, you know.

— Henrik Ibsen, *The Wild Duck*, Act 5

Oleg had a spitting habit back then.

"You kids know what crabs are?" Nikolai Khernofsky, Oleg's uncle — the chef, waiter, *and* owner of Nicky's Diner — asked, elbows resting on the wooden restaurant counter. "Not the kind you could eat, kids. No, no, no. Vicious creatures, these ones."

There was only one fry left on the white oval plate in front of Nikolai, and Charlie Crouse, reaching for it with his right hand, standing up from his blue-topped bar stool, grabbed it and stuffed it into his mouth. "I know what they are, Mr. Khernofsky," he said, chewing. "They're little bugs that eat your crotch."

"And how do these bugs get in your pants, kid?"

"If you stick your dick somewhere dirty."

"Holy mackerel!" Nikolai smacked a palm on the counter. "How do you know that, kid? What are you — nine, ten years old?"

"Twelve."

"Twelve? Well, let me tell you," Nikolai said, addressing only Oleg and me. "This kid, this is a —" He turned back to Charlie. "What's your name again?"

"Charlie."

"Farley," Nikolai repeated with pride, turned back to us. "Farley's a smart kid, boys. He knows, ha, he knows something about safety. How come I never met this kid before, Oleg? This is a smart kid. You and Jimmy, sometimes you are not so smart. But this kid —" He plopped a hand on Charlie's shoulder, nodded at him. "This is a smart kid. How about some more fries, eh? These are the best in Toronto, Farley. The finest."

"It's Charlie."

"Sure. Charlie. But listen. You listening, kid?"

"Yes."

Nikolai looked him hard in the eye, tightened his grip. "If you taste some better fries anywhere else in this city … if you taste some better fries than these, Farley, I'll … I'll eat my pants!" He let go of Charlie's shoulder, clasped his hands together. "Ha, ha! Every last scrap of them, in my belly!"

Later that day, after our house-league basketball game at Saint Joseph's Community Centre, the three of us strolled a few blocks west to Korea Town, and like most Sunday afternoons blew whatever change we had at the Fun Village Arcade, a modest place on the first floor of an old three-storey red-brick building on Bloor Street.

As soon as we got inside, Oleg — the star of our ball game, raking in thirty-two points (more than half the team's total score)

— planted himself on one of the orange swervy-bottomed plastic chairs in the front section of the place and popped a quarter into the mini-arcade machine resting on the green table in front of him. There were three in Fun Village, boxy things that for a quarter offered games like sports trivia, memory, touch and shoot basketball, and the most popular — the only game anybody really used them for — virtual strip poker.

Oleg picked his regular model, a tall, big-eyed blonde wearing an elegant black dress and black high heels, who always began the card game sitting cross-legged on a red plush armchair in a bookshelf-lined room which, a pink-lettered caption above her photograph revealed, was her husband's study.

Her name — the caption also let her challenger know before the game of poker started — was Sylvia Broomdale, and her hobbies included shopping, driving sports cars, astrology, and being naughty while her husband was away on business.

"Bet you don't even get her shoes off," Charlie said, and I followed him into the back of the arcade, dimly lit, dusty, where all the real games were. The big ones. The monsters. Taller than we were, at least twelve of them, lofty, dark, looming machines with blinking screens ringing out sound effects: Marvel vs. Capcom, Raiden, Tekken, Bust a Move, and, Charlie's favourite — probably because nobody could beat him at it — Mike Tyson 2000.

Charlie slipped a quarter into the lit-up orange slot. "You ready to get pounded, Jim?" he asked.

As an animated referee announced our fighters (I was Tyson, Charlie was Lennox Lewis), we waited for our match to begin. Like always when he was concentrating hard on something, Charlie's face went slack and his mouth drooped a bit, which made him resemble a two-year-old, mesmerized, gazing at a dog for the first time.

Then the referee said, "Let's keep it clean!" a bell sounded, the crowd cheered, and the fight began. After violently jerking our joysticks back and forth and pushing down the two blue and red buttons with hyperactive speed for a minute and a half, Lennox Lewis unleashed a combo (two left jabs, a right hook, then a left uppercut), and Tyson, jelly-legged, stumbled back against the ropes, struggled to stay on his feet for a brief moment, then fell to the floor, where he lay motionless during the ten count. Yellow birdies circled over his head.

"I'm the heavyweight champion of the world!" Charlie crowed. "The King! The King!"

Oleg — I could only see his profile from where I was in the back of the arcade — was still stooped over on the orange chair, trying his luck with Mrs. Broomdale.

"Got her socks off yet?" Charlie hollered over to him.

Then, just as Oleg was about to yell something back, George, the owner of Fun Village Arcade — stringy, fiftyish, Italian, always wore the same red golf shirt with a green collar — stomped up to him from behind his counter. George was red-faced, trembling, and had a black Louisville Slugger firmly gripped in his right hand.

"You think-a-you live here, huh?" he demanded in a shaky, high-pitched voice, standing over Oleg.

Oleg had a spitting habit back then. You'd walk with him down the sidewalk and he'd stop at every crack, tilt his head toward the ground, and aim a glob of spit in between. He'd spit at street signs and stop signs. From his second-floor bedroom above Nicky's Diner he'd launch spit out his window onto passing cars and pedestrians below. He'd spit on the basketball court at Kingston Park after every shot he made. He'd spit at pigeons and squirrels, wandering cats, dogs, raccoons. He'd spit in your house if you didn't watch out. Couldn't go two minutes without hoarking or dribbling some kind of saliva out of his mouth.

"Huh?" George croaked, and with his free hand undid the top button of his golf shirt, exposing a bundle of wiry brown chest hair. "You think-a-you live here?"

Oleg stared straight ahead, chalk-white.

Everybody in the arcade — there were only six of us; the other three were Korean kids with dyed red bangs — had turned their attention George's way. Never before had I seen him fuss about the cleanliness of his business. It wasn't a clean place, especially the floor: the green-and-white-checkered linoleum was dusty and cracked, littered with cigarette ash and Pepsi stains. It looked as if it hadn't been washed in years. Probably hadn't been washed in years. Probably had never been washed.

The George we knew was passive, lazy, spent his work hours leaning back on the white plastic lawn chair behind his counter, feet up, watching soccer games and Italian sitcoms on the small, fuzzy-screened television set he'd placed atop three grey milk crates in the corner of the room. Now and then he'd laugh real hard at something he saw on the TV, but other than that he rarely opened his mouth. You asked him to give you quarters for your loonie — he opened up his cash register, took four quarters out, and dropped them into your hand. You ordered a beef patty — he fetched one out of the oven, wrapped a napkin around it, and put it on the counter. Nothing more.

"You gonna act like-a-that? Like-a-some dog … like-a-some *dog*?" George bent down to Oleg's level, looked him hard in the eye. "You gonna act like-a-some *dog* in your mother's … *your mother's* … your mother's own house, huh?"

Oleg was a statue.

Small drops of sweat were sliding down George's cheek, along his stubbly neck, and into his chest hair, making it glisten. "Huh?" he screeched, and smacked the tip of his bat against the small puddle of saliva on the floor next to Oleg's orange chair.

"You gonna act like-a-that, huh? You gonna act like-a-some dog, like-a —"

"No," Oleg said.

George opened his mouth to say something but seemed to forget why he had confronted Oleg in the first place and just stared at him, lips hanging apart, dumbfounded.

"No," Oleg repeated, appearing as if he were trying to hold back a sneeze.

The whole place was quiet save for the electronic jingles coming from the arcade machines.

Then George stood straight, took a step back from Oleg. "No?" he said. "This is no your house, huh?" He flung an arm in the air, indicating the whole arcade. "You no gonna spit like-a-some dog in your house?"

"No," Oleg said.

"No?"

"No."

"Huh?" George said, smacking the barrel of his bat into his empty palm. "What's you gonna tell me?"

"This isn't my house," Oleg said, still staring straight ahead.

"No. This is *no* your house."

"No," Oleg said.

"You gonna spit in my house?"

Oleg peered up at George. "You live here?" He wasn't trying to be a smartass. It was just a stupid, nervous question, but it was the wrong thing to say, because George grinned widely when Oleg said this, wrapped his free hand around the Louisville Slugger, choked up the way kids do in little league, and took a fierce swing — an aimed-to-kill swing — at Oleg's head.

Oleg dodged backward just in time so that the bat missed his ear by an inch and smashed straight into the screen of the mini-arcade box, spraying plastic and bits of wire all over the floor.

"You see, huh, what's-a-gonna happen when you have no respect?" George bellowed wildly, regaining his batting stance. "You see, huh, what's-a-gonna happen, huh, when you spit like-a-some-dog in somebody house, huh?"

Oleg was trapped against the wall, turned sideways to protect his crotch, hands shielding his face.

"Huh?" George roared. "You see what's-a-gonna happen!" And he took another swing, vertical this time, as if he were chopping wood.

Oleg stretched his body flat against the wall and sucked in his stomach. The tip of the bat grazed his brown T-shirt and drove hard into the orange chair. George stumbled forward from the force of his monster swing, and Oleg, grasping the opportunity — as swift as Pinball Clemons dodging a tackle — slid past him and bolted out the front door.

George didn't chase him. He watched him exit. Watched the door swing shut. Then he turned back to the green table, breathed in deeply through his nose, and took another swing, this time aiming at the arcade box, and knocked what was left of it onto the floor.

"What's-a-gonna-happen, huh?" he whispered to himself, gazing at the broken, tangled, buzzing machine sombrely, flushed, as if it was his pet dog he'd just beaten. Then he turned to the kids in the back. "Get out."

Stunned from the whole fiasco, we didn't move.

"Get out!" he repeated with more volume, and before we had time to go anywhere, he was chasing everyone toward the front door, swinging his bat like a madman, threatening to murder all of our mothers and grandmothers and sisters and daughters if we ever stepped foot in his business again.

The next Sunday, after our house-league basketball game at Saint Joseph's Community Centre, the three of us returned to

Fun Village Arcade. George didn't so much as raise an eyebrow. Oleg — he'd just reached a season high, scoring fifty-six points — cautiously walked up to the counter and asked George to change his loonie for four quarters. Like a robot, without taking his eyes off the TV, George popped open his cash register, reached in, picked out four quarters, and dropped them into Oleg's hand.

Charlie nudged my shoulder, winked, then hoarked a thick green loogie onto the floor. "Stupid wop," he whispered, and we walked to the back of the arcade to play a game of Tekken, one-on-one martial-arts combat.

Only half, darling.

"Hell you looking at, buddy?"

No answer.

"What, you don't speak English? No speak-ee, you?"

Run. Run away.

"Huh? No speak-ee?"

He was leaning against the outside of the school, next to the front entrance, a navy blue San Diego Padres cap tipped back on his head. He'd been glaring at every kid who walked out the door. Why'd he have to pick me to start with? I could swear I only glanced his way.

"You in the special class or something?"

"No."

"Then how come you can't answer a question?"

He swaggered up to the front steps, hands jammed into pockets. I stood still, fists clenched, anticipating a blow. But he didn't touch me. Just stared at my forehead for about fifteen seconds as if there was a purple growth the size of a baseball sticking from it. Then he asked, "You go to school here?"

It was the first day of grade seven at Lawson Street Junior High. Oleg, my only friend, had gone to a different school.

"Yeah," I said.

"Me, too."

"You do?"

"No, I'm lying to you." He shook his head, rolled his eyes. "The hell else would I be doing outside this place?"

"Dunno."

"Shit, if I didn't have to go to class, I wouldn't walk in a ten-mile radius of this stupid building. You know it used to be a jail, right?"

"What?"

"This building, it used to be a jail. You knew that, right?"

"No."

"You didn't know that? I thought everybody knew that. Ten years back it was a maximum-security jail, this school."

"Yeah?"

"You really didn't know that, eh? Man, oh, man. I forget sometimes how stupid some people are. Our school, buddy, is where they threw all the craziest serial killers. The worst ones. Guys that chopped up their wives, raped their pets. And they all used to sleep in our classrooms. Used to lift weights in the playground. And also they chucked Mafia and skinheads and all types of serious gang members in there, too. People got stabbed in those hallways every day. Had to have somebody go around

and clean up the blood with a mop … every day. And i
maximum security, right, so they used to have guards armed
with machine guns surrounding the place. And there was a fifty-
foot barbed wire fence, and they put a force field on the fence,
and if you touched it, you got an electric shock so bad you'd be
paralyzed for a week … or maybe two weeks, depending on how
strong you were. But, man, oh, man, I don't believe you didn't
know about the jail. I thought everybody knew about that."

"Oh."

He stared at me for about ten seconds as if I had the words
I AM A MORON written with pink marker on my forehead. Then
he said, "You know I'm joking, right?"

"What?"

"This place wasn't a jail, buddy."

"Oh."

"The hell would anybody put a jail downtown like this?
That'd probably be the stupidest idea in the world. This area is
full of houses. What kind of idiot would wanna live around here
if there was a maximum-security jail across the street?"

"Dunno."

"You believed me, though."

"No."

"Yeah, you did. Don't lie. You thought this school used to
be a jail. I bet you were gonna go home and tell your mommy
you wanna transfer schools 'cause you're afraid the ghost of
some pedophile is gonna sneak up on you when you go to take
a piss. I bet you woulda stayed awake all night if I hadn't told
you I was joking. I saw the way you were looking at me. You
believed me."

"No."

"Don't lie."

"I'm not."

"Whatever, you stupid dumbass. It's not my fault you're an idiot."

"But I didn't —"

"The hell were you staring at me before?"

"What? I wasn't."

"You were staring at me when you walked out the door. The hell were you looking at?"

"Nothing. I wasn't. I mean, I didn't think I … You were staring at everybody that walked out the door."

"That's 'cause I'm waiting for somebody."

"Oh."

"It's important who I'm waiting for."

"Oh."

"Don't you wanna know who it is?"

"Who?"

"None of your business."

"Oh."

He scratched his chin for a little while, glanced at the ground. "Well, it's a girl I'm waiting for. This sexy girl. Probably missed her, though. I told her to meet me here around two-thirty 'cause I figured I could get out of school early behind a teacher's back. But none of the teachers would let me leave my desk, not even to take a piss. Place might as well be a jail. But, anyway, she probably came already and thought I stood her up. It's a shame 'cause last time I saw her she let me take a peek down her panties."

"Yeah?"

"You think I'm gonna lie about something like that? That's the third time she's let me see it."

"Really?"

"She got red pubes."

"Red?"

"Same colour as her hair."

"Where were you?"

"What, when she showed me?"

"Yeah," I said.

"None of your business."

"Oh."

He kicked a pebble, watched it roll. "Well, first time was on the train tracks. By Dupont, you know?"

"Yeah."

"I took her walking down there, and right when a train went by, she stretched her panties out so I could look down."

"She did that?"

"Swear to God."

"For how long?"

"Till the train passed all the way. As soon as the train passed and the noise was gone, she didn't let me look no more. It was a long train, though. So, I don't know, probably a minute, two minutes, I seen it for.

"*Holy.*"

"Said she might let me touch it this time. You ever touched one?"

"What?"

"A twat. Pussy."

"No."

"But you've seen one, right?"

"A real one?"

"Yeah. On a real girl. A girl who showed it to you."

"Dunno."

"That means no. You should try and see one. A real one, I mean."

"How many real ones you seen?"

He furrowed his brow, as if he were calculating in his head. "'Bout fifty."

"*Fifty?*"

"Yeah, 'bout that. But, anyway, I figure this girl I was waiting for ain't gonna show up. You know what a whore is, buddy?"

"Like a hooker?"

"Yeah, a hooker. A whore."

"Yeah, I know what that is."

"You ever seen one before?"

"Not really."

"What do you mean *not really?*"

There was this Coffee Time near my house — at the edge of my street turn west on Bloor, walk three blocks, you were there — and if you passed by after midnight, you'd normally see at least one car pulled into a far corner of the parking lot with somebody in the driver's seat, and if you looked closely at the driver, you'd notice there was something furry, dark, could be some kind of animal, moving up and down on his lap, and if you peered even closer, maybe snuck a few feet toward the car to get a better view, you'd realize that the dark, furry thing had a neck, two ears, a whole body, and if you got any closer, the guy in the driver's seat would probably roll down his window and tell you to screw off and mind your own business before he got out of the car and punched your face in, you little pervert.

"I mean, I've seen one. Passed by one on the —"

"Yeah, whatever," he said. "You wanna see a real one?"

"Where?"

"I know a place. She won't come out till later, though. Time is it?"

My Timex said four-thirteen. "Quarter past four."

"You gotta go home for dinner?"

"I think so. Yeah."

"Your parents would let you come out afterward?"

"Yeah, I could come out."

"So then meet me back here at six-thirty."

"Six-thirty?"

"You didn't hear me the first time?"

"I heard you."

"Then the hell's wrong with you?"

"What?"

"You're retarded, eh?"

"No."

"What's your name?"

"Jim ... Jim Myers," I said.

"I'm Charlie."

"Oh."

"Retard," Charlie mumbled, then crossed the road, slipping between idle traffic, and headed south down a side street. I walked west, back to my house on Concord Avenue.

My kitchen: a square white-walled room with white cabinets and a white counter and a white Bosche dishwasher and a white gas stove and a white table with four wooden chairs and a white fridge that had a white rectangular magnet sticking to the top left corner that read DR. R. BRUSILOFF GENERAL IMPLANT AND DENTISTRY in black print and below that had the address (somewhere on St. Clair Avenue West) and the telephone number (I knew it started with a nine) of Dr. R. Brusiloff's office. Black and white tiles on the floor. Track lighting on the ceiling.

The sole piece of art in the room was a framed watercolour on the wall across from the sink that my sister, Amanda, had brought home the first summer she came back to Toronto from Queen's University in Kingston, Ontario. It was a semi-bird's-eye view of a dense pine forest that cut off into a glassy green lake, with the sun setting all purple and pink on the horizon.

Marcia, Amanda's dorm mate during her first year of university — who Amanda said was pretty much like her twin, they
had so much in common — had painted the watercolour at the
family cottage in Muskoka (where Amanda had spent reading
week) and given it to Amanda for her nineteenth birthday.

When I returned home from my first day of school at Lawson
Street Junior High, Amanda — she was taking a bus back to
Kingston the next morning to begin her second year of university
— was standing in the kitchen, admiring Marcia's watercolour
from a few steps back, three fingers pushed into her cheek.

"Isn't it just ... beautiful, Jim?" she asked without taking her
eyes off the picture. "Don't you think it adds a lot to this room?
Makes it a lot more, I don't know ... livable?"

I flung my knapsack onto the floor, looked at the painting.

"It's the ... colours," she said. "Marcia has such a good sense
of colour. There's something about them that's so perfect ... so
real ... in a way ... but not real. So ... imperfect ..."

"Imperfect?"

"Yes, Jim. Imperfect."

"Oh."

"Imperfect," she whispered to herself, and stood there, neck
hunched, chin up, knees locked, small belly pushing against her
floral-patterned button-down blouse, gazing deeply into the
watercolour as if she were trying to find Waldo, until I asked her
— and this was an honest inquiry — how come she didn't hang
the picture in her room if she liked it so much.

My sister huffed loudly and turned to me. Her face was
long, and she had a small, squishy nose like my father's, a bum
chin, tiny eyes, straight brown hair with blond streaks bunched
together at the back of her head with a see-through plastic clip.
She gazed at me in that I-know-something-you-don't way she
had of making her chin wrinkle and her upper lip touch her

nostrils. Instead of answering my question, she turned back to the watercolour, stared at it silently for a few moments, then, still looking at the picture, told me that Marcia had spent the summer sleeping on the uneven giant-cockroach-ridden dirt floor of a thatched hut in a small, impoverished West African village helping to build a library with a youth organization, and she wished she had done something interesting like that with her summer, something meaningful, something challenging, something ... altruistic. *Altruistic.* Did I know what that word meant?

"No," I said, and instead of telling me what that word meant, Amanda scratched the back of her neck, made a face as if she'd just taken a sip of rotten milk, and told me how much it sucked being stuck in nothing-to-do Toronto all summer working as a stupid lifeguard at stupid Sunnyside Pool, and how she hated the guy who worked with her, just hated him. He was this annoying high-school kid who called himself G-Bone, and he was cocky and talked as if he was black even though he was skinny and white and was so ignorant about everything, so affected, so uninformed, so ... high school. And it was a stupid idea to take the job, and when she thinks about it the only *real* reason why she worked here all summer was because she felt as if she had to be around the house, that it wasn't fair for her to be away all the time, the way our father was so ... *old.* Seventy-one. Could I believe Dad was seventy-one?

"I guess," I said.

"He was sixteen at the end of World War II."

"I know."

"He walks with a cane."

"I know."

"It's hard for him to get to the second floor sometimes."

"I know."

"He has dentures."

"I know," I said.

Amanda smiled at me in an older-sister-kind-of-way, cocking her head a little, peering at me as if I were still an infant, and told me again how miserable it was being stuck in Toronto, especially knowing there was *sooo* much to see in this world, *soooo* much to do, *sooooo* much to learn, *soooooo* many interesting people to meet, and how wonderful it would be to travel around Europe or South America or Asia for a year, and her and Marcia were planning to go on some kind of trip after they graduated but that was still a long way away and she didn't want to start thinking too far ahead because you never knew how things were going to turn out, and I should always remember that, that you never knew how things were going to turn out.

"You don't?"

"No," she said, then turned back to the watercolour, made a face as if somebody were shining a flashlight in her eyes, and said that living in Kingston last year, being independent, going to university — all of that was a really good experience. She couldn't wait to leave tomorrow and move into the five-room apartment she'd found with Marcia and this other girl named Deborah who lived on her dorm floor during first year. Deb was from Ottawa and was really funny, said the most random things, and the three of them got along really well. They were all pretty much like twins, triplets, really, and she knew she'd already told me about Deb a hundred times. It was just that she was really excited for everything, especially her courses. They all looked super-interesting and stimulating, and the professors all seemed *sooooo* smart ... and one of them was really young, still in his twenties, she thought.

"What courses you take?" I asked.

"Mostly soshe."

"Soshe?"

"Sociology, Jim."

"Oh," I said.

Amanda walked to the fridge, opened the door, slouched down, and peered inside. Her grey sweatpants were riding low, and you could see the white elastic on her underwear pressing against the chubby pale skin where her back began, a few inches below where her blouse cut.

"Where's Dad?" I asked.

"He's asleep."

"Oh."

Amanda bent down farther, scanning the bottom shelves, and her sweatpants slid lower on her hips, making more of her underwear visible. Baby blue. Cotton.

"I gotta go then," I said.

She turned around, let the fridge door swing shut. "You're going?"

"Yeah, I gotta go … with Oleg. Play some ball in the alley."

"Well, okay, Jim." She walked toward me. "My bus leaves early tomorrow morning, so I probably won't see you for a while. You'll come visit me, right?"

"Yes."

"Oh, Jim," she gushed, and gave me a quick, tight hug, pulling my head into her bosom, then pushing it away.

Her blouse smelled like baby powder. Then she held on to my shoulders for a minute or so, looking into my eyes. I thought maybe she was going to cry. But suddenly her gaze dropped from my face and hovered directly below my belly. She stared at the small bulge for half a second, then, realizing it wasn't piss showing through my light blue jeans, she whipped her hands violently from my shoulders, opened her mouth to speak — or scream, or vomit, or *laugh* — but I ran out of the kitchen before I could see which one it was. Ten seconds later I was jogging east through an alleyway, back toward the front entrance of Lawson Street Junior High.

Somebody was strangling me. An arm. Wrapped around my neck. Cutting my breath. Probably some homicidal maniac. No point fighting him, though. Too strong. I was a goner. Goodbye. Wouldn't take long. Just let myself go. Don't fight. Don't scream. Couldn't scream. Jeez, it was easy to die …

But suddenly the grip loosened, and Charlie was standing in front of me outside the entrance of Lawson Street Junior High, a half-finished cigarette hanging from his lips, feet turned out like a duck's.

"Oh," I said.

He took the smoke out of his mouth, ashed on the sidewalk. "You're an idiot, you know that?"

"What?"

"I said meet me here at six-thirty."

"So I came early."

"What you do that for?"

"Dunno. Forgot which time."

"You're retarded, eh?"

"What? How … well, how come you came so early?"

"How come I came so early?"

"Yeah."

He took a drag off his cigarette, blew the smoke in my face. "This girl kicked me out of her house."

"You went and saw that girl?"

"No, a different one. This girl I know from my old school. Georgia. But she kicked me out when her mom came home. Made me climb out her window."

"Yeah?"

"Swear to God. She was naked, too."

"Her mom?"

"No, you idiot. The girl. I had her naked. Well, everything but her socks. She kept those on 'cause I told her to. But all her other clothes — bra, panties, all that — she stripped them off in front of me. In her room."

"She did that?"

"Buddy, I'm gonna lie about something like that? Course, she stripped for me. This girl loves to strip for me. She puts on some music and does it like a stripper, teasing me and shit, dangling the panties down her legs and all that."

"Yeah?"

"We were probably gonna screw, too, but then her mom came home, so I had to bolt."

"You were gonna *screw*?"

"Course. But her mom'll smack her hard if she catches a boy in the house, so I had to get out of there."

"So you didn't go home for dinner then?"

"Nah. Not today. I figured I'd just come by here after she kicked me out and hang around till you showed up. *If* you showed up. I didn't think you were gonna show up."

"How come?"

"'Cause you're a retard."

"Oh."

He took another pull off his cigarette, then flicked the butt onto the road. "So you wanna see this whore or what?"

"Yeah."

"Scared?"

"No."

I followed Charlie south through an alleyway, kicking pebbles and learning a lot more about Georgia and this other girl from his old school — Caroline, a Filipina, four years

older than us, who had a piercing on her vagina and liked
to screw so much she waited in a park by Yonge Street every
Friday night and gave it to the first guy who came up to her,
no matter who he was.

"Even if," I said, "I don't know ... like if he had warts all over
his neck and his chin?"

"I told you," Charlie said. "No matter who he is." Then he
proceeded to tell me about the time Caroline had invited him
to her house, the things they'd begun to do in her bedroom,
and was just about to say what happened after her one-eyed
older brother, a member of an infamously violent Filipino gang,
barged through the door with a machete in his hand, when we
came to a green dumpster in the alleyway.

We'd been walking for about a half-hour.

"This is the spot," Charlie said, strolling up to the dumpster,
which was in front of a criss-crossed metal fence, maybe six
feet high.

"But wait," I said. "So he cut you or what?"

"I'll tell you another time."

"What do you mean? C'mon. What happened? You get sliced?"

"I said I'll tell you another time."

"You had to fight him or what?"

"Shut up!" Charlie snapped. He hoisted his body on top of
the dumpster and dangled over the fence, hanging from the
top bar, then dropped onto the other side, where there was a
small concrete yard that led to a flat-topped grey-brick building, two storeys high, with a fire escape zigzagging to the roof.
Crouching down like a soldier, Charlie snuck across the yard
and started climbing the fire escape.

Halfway up the black metal stairs, he turned my way (I was
still on the other side of the fence), shook his head, then continued toward the top.

By the time I made it over the fence, Charlie was already on the roof. When I got up to the roof, he was lying on his belly by the edge and staring down at the sidewalk.

"That's her," he said.

I lay down next to him.

"Probably screws fifty guys a night."

"Yeah?"

"Maybe more."

"She could do that?"

"Buddy, that's her job."

We could only see her backside. She was facing the road, leaning against a street light, arms and ankles crossed. Doughnut-size silver hoops hung from each ear, and it seemed as if their weight was pulling her head to the ground, hunching her whole body forward.

"She Chinese, you think?"

"She's Asian," Charlie said. "But she ain't Chinese. From Japan. Know how I can tell?"

"How?"

"She's tall, right. Probably almost six feet."

"So?"

"So it's impossible for a Chinese girl to grow that much. There's never been one taller than five eight in all of history. Never. The only Asian girls that could grow taller than that are the ones from Japan."

"Really?"

"Swear on my balls. You could look it up in any encyclopedia."

She seemed thirty-five, maybe forty years old, and had on a glittery pink tube top, a tight cheetah-skin-patterned skirt, and red knee-high boots made from material that if I hadn't known better might think was strawberry Fruit Roll-Up. Her hair was paintbrush-black and was pulled back into a slick-tight ponytail.

"And she just … she … you think you gotta be a certain age or something to … you know … to …"

"Screw her?"

"Yeah."

"Hell, no," Charlie said. "As long as you got the dough, she'll give you the goods. Could be six years old — doesn't matter. If you fork over the cash, she'll do whatever you tell her. There ain't any rules or anything like that. You give her the money, she gives you the goods. Simple."

"But what if your face was all burnt up or something?"

"What?"

"I don't know," I said. "Like, if you were in a fire and you ended up burning most of the skin off your face … and all that was left was scars. Even your lips. She'd still do you if your face was like that … even if you gave her the dough?"

"Man, oh, man."

"What?"

"You are retarded, eh?"

"What?"

"Sure she'd screw you if your face was all burnt!"

"Really?"

"Of course!"

"It's the same for all of them?"

"Pretty much."

"How much then … how much it usually cost, you think?"

"For a whore?"

"Yeah."

"Depends," Charlie said. "Some cost up to three, four hundred bucks. Some you could even pay, like, five, six grand. There's this one girl in L.A. costs two million for one night. *Two million.* But with an older broad like this, I'd say somewhere around —"

"Fifty!" hollered a deep, patient-sounding female voice.

It felt as if the word had been whipped into my mouth and gotten stuck going down my throat, and now there was this awful lump jammed right above my Adam's apple.

"Fifty dollars," the woman repeated. Then she turned fully around, and she *was* Asian, from Korea, maybe, and her breasts were all shoved together and popping out of her bubblegum-pink tube top. You could see right down the dark crevice between them because she was staring up at us from beside the street light, hands pressing against her hips.

"Think I don't hear you whispering up there?" She made a mouth with her fingers. "*Chat, chat, chat, chat, chat.* I got ears, right? I could hear you up there. I know what you want, right? Fifty dollars. You don't get a better deal than that, right? Never. That's the best price you'll get. Wait till you —" She glanced over her shoulder as if to make sure nobody was around. Nobody was around. "Wait till you see what I can do for fifty dollars. Come down here and let me show you what I can do. Fifty dollars. You want me or what?"

She stood in the middle of the sidewalk, looking up at us, waiting for a reply.

There was no reply.

"C'mon, you two mutes all of sudden? What's wrong?"

We were mutes all of a sudden.

"Don't be afraid, boys. I'm not … I'm not gonna hurt you. There's nothing to be afraid of."

Charlie smacked my arm. "She thinks we're *scared*?"

I didn't answer.

"You think we're scared?" he blurted down at her, his voice shaky.

She seemed much older and more tired as we got closer. She was leaning against the street light, facing the road, her ankles and arms crossed — the exact way she'd been standing when we were on the roof. Charlie was two steps ahead of me, moving

slowly, cautiously, as if he were approaching a growling pit bull.
Her cheetah-skin-patterned skirt had a silver zipper going up
the side, undone halfway, and you could see part of what she was
wearing underneath, something yellow.

We were only a few feet away when she turned and smiled
grimly, rolling her eyes, as if one of us had told her a really cheesy
joke. "Name's Martina Hingis." She took a step forward. Her face
was much wider than it appeared from the roof, all powdered
and pale save for a smear of turquoise above each eye and her
eggplant-purple lips.

"Joe," Charlie said.

"Well, hello, Joe," she said, then turned to me. "Let me guess
—" she pressed a finger against her chin "— Bob, right? Or wait,
no ... Bill? Fred? No, it's Frank, right? You're Frank. Frank's your
name, isn't it?"

"Oleg," I said.

"Oleg ..." She seemed impressed. "Well, that's quite a name.
That's what, Russian? Russian, are you?"

"Yeah."

"I knew a girl from Russia." She glanced at an empty Coke
can lying on the sidewalk in front of her, re-crossed her arms.
"Jumped on the tracks at Osgoode subway station, but the train
didn't kill her. Didn't even break a leg. She believed in ghosts,
the crazy girl. She was a sweetie, though. But *ghosts* ..." She
squinted at the label on the Coke can as if she were trying to
read the small white print listing the ingredients.

Charlie and I waited for her to say something more, but she
didn't. She stayed like that for a half-minute or so. Then Charlie
said, "You okay over there, miss?"

"But I believed her," Martina said, raising her eyebrows —
toothpick-skinny black arcs, painted on. "Ever since she told me
about her grandfather, I believed in ghosts."

Charlie flashed me a funny look.

She turned to me. "You're Russian, right?" She said that as if the fact should make clear what she was talking about.

"Yeah."

"Well," she said. "I knew a Russian girl who believed in ghosts."

"Oh."

"Forget it," she said. "You don't … forget it."

Then she walked up to Charlie, bent down to his height (she was about two and a half heads taller), and grinned at him in the same kind of lusty way Oleg's older brother sometimes grinned at Oleg before he busted him in the face, or grabbed one of his nipples, twisted, *then* busted him in the face.

"Fifty dollars," she said, breasts — softball size with freckled leathery tops — right under Charlie's chin. "We could do whatever you want. I'll do whatever."

"Thing is, I only got —"

"Fifty dollars," she said again, louder this time. "I'll take you right over there." She nodded at the alleyway we'd walked out of. "We don't gotta go anywhere far. I like you. You're sexy. Your friend, too. Little hunks. I bet you guys know how to —"

"I only got twenty."

Martina rolled her eyes. "Twenty? That's it?"

"Yeah."

"Let's see it."

"What? Why you need to see it?"

"Listen," she said, voice suddenly firm, "if you're gonna act funny, you can scram."

"What?"

She stood back up, towering over Charlie. "I need the money first. Those are the rules, kid. No money up front and you can hit the road." She stuck out an open palm.

Charlie stared at it.

"I don't got time for cheapies, right?" she said. "Like yester-day, right? This short guy, this Paki, wouldn't shut up. 'The last prophet's the only right one,' he said. 'Muhammad's the last prophet. Muhammad's this and that. You have to follow the last prophet, right, because that's the way it goes, right? When a new one comes along, he's the proper one. Jesus, Moses, Abraham — they're all too old. Their time's passed, right? Muhammad's the only real prophet for our time. Muhammad, Muhammad, Muhammad. The newest one. Don't believe what anybody else says. Pray to Allah. Listen to Muhammad. Somebody tells you something else, it's wrong. I know the truth. Blah, blah, blah, blah, blah.' Cheapie Paki didn't have a penny. Wouldn't leave me alone, right? Just wanted to yak my ear off. I don't got time for that." She glared at Charlie, palm out. Her face was like an angry bird's. "You gonna pay or scram?"

Charlie raised his chin. "How about if I —"

"Pay or scram, kid?"

"All right, all right," Charlie said. Warily, he took a crumpled twenty out of his pocket and placed it in her hand.

She stuffed the bill in her handbag.

"So, like, we could do —" Charlie began.

"Don't worry, kid," she said, zipping up her bag. "Whatever you want. We'll have lots of fun. Buckets … buckets of fun." She snorted, turned to me. "What about you. What's in your pockets?"

I shook my head.

"You forgot how to speak?"

"No."

"Then let's see."

"See what?"

"Show me what's in your pockets."

"Oh. There's nothing. Nothing."

"Then show me."

I didn't understand.

"Empty your pockets, kid."

"Oh," I said, pulling the lining out of my pockets.

She looked at each one closely, sticking her neck forward. They were empty save for my back-door key. "Cheapie," she muttered, then turned to Charlie. "Twenty's all you got, huh?"

"Yeah."

"So if I checked in your wallet right now there wouldn't be a penny?"

"You don't believe me?"

"If I checked in your wallet, there wouldn't be a penny?"

"No."

"Then show me."

"What?"

"Show me your wallet, kid. I wanna see if you're messing with me."

"I'm not."

"Then show me."

"I ain't showing you my wallet," Charlie said.

"'Cause you got more dough, right? Lousy cheapie. Trying to rip —"

"No."

"Why not then?"

"'Cause I don't want you touching my wallet."

"Oh," she said, throwing her hands in the air, "so you'll trust me with your cock in my hand but not your money, eh? Want me to touch your little pee-pee but not your wallet, right? Ha! If I were you, kid, I'd be lots more afraid of the damage I could do with your —"

"Screw this," Charlie said. "Give me back the twenty, miss.

I don't want nothing from you. Forget it." Switching roles, he stuck out his palm.

She ignored it. "Won't even fork over fifty for the best there is! Bet you buy your sneakers at Value Village, you misers, you … you stupid cheapie kids! Think I'm gonna give it up for nothing, right? Give you each a freebie? You think I'm gonna —"

"Listen, just give me the —"

"Six hundred, one fella pays!" She sliced her arm through the air. "Six hundred dollars! Just for an hour. Six hundred for one hour! That's big time. More than a lawyer makes. And I work for myself. Every penny goes in my pocket. That's real money. I make real money. I buy nice things. Prada, Gucci — all that shit! And you think I got time to give you two —"

"We don't want nothing, lady. Just give me my money back and we'll —"

"Lousy cheapskates!" she hissed, twirled around, and began strutting away from us down the sidewalk. "Misers! Cheapers! Cheapsters …"

"I ain't leaving you alone till I get my money," Charlie said, trying to catch up.

"You're gonna walk me home?"

"If I have to."

She didn't answer, kept walking. I was following, too, a little way behind Charlie.

"You think I'm stupid, lady?" Charlie said. "Give me the money."

"Don't got it."

Charlie sped up. "What?"

"You never gave me shit, kid. Nothing. Never paid me nothing. Don't know what you're talking about. You're talking non-sense. Trying to rip me off." She took longer strides. "Now get outta here. Quit bothering me. Go to bed."

Charlie ran up beside her. "You think you're gonna rob me, lady? Give me the money."

Again she picked up her pace. "Scram, kid."

Charlie matched her speed. "Give it."

"Dunno what you're talking about, kid."

"C'mon, lady. Enough of this. I gave you my twenty. Hand it over."

She gained a step on him. "It's past your bedtime. Go home. Your mother's probably wondering where —"

"You stupid whore! You ugly ... you ..."

She stopped, didn't turn around, waited.

Crying.

She must be crying. Sobbing silently, a hand over her mouth, eyes squeezed shut the way my sister did for three weeks straight after being dumped by her first boyfriend.

But when the hooker turned around and looked down at Charlie, her face was dry and she was smiling, squinty-eyed, cheeks all bunched up as if he were a dressed-up little girl or a cute-eyed kitten. She put her hands on her knees, again crouched to Charlie's height, and said, as if he were an old friend of hers, "Used to sleep in her bathtub, right, 'cause she figured it was the only safe place in her apartment. Her bathtub. She put a mattress in her bathtub, right? Pillow, blanket, everything. Figured there were ghosts in all the other rooms, right, and they'd get her at night, so she sleeps in the bathtub. Tub's the only place she feels safe, right? And her home's in Russia. Has no family in Toronto. She's the only person in her family to ever leave the country, right? And listen, one night she's about to go to bed and she sees something buried in the plaster on her bathroom wall, a piece of paper or something, right? So she digs it out, and it's a photograph. It's her grandfather. It's a picture of her grandfather who never left Russia. His picture's buried in the wall of her apartment. In her bathroom. In Toronto. How did it get there, eh? She showed me the picture, too — this old, wrinkled guy with no hair. Says she's a hundred percent sure it's him. And I believe her. It makes sense, right? The only place she feels safe sleeping, and there's this picture of her grandfather buried in the wall. Like he's protecting her and she could sense it. Spooky, eh?"

"The hell you talking about lady?"

"I didn't used to believe in nothing like that." She shook her head to animate the point. "Aliens, zombies, ghosts, spirits — all that *X-Files* junk. But ever since she told me about her grandfather, I believed in ghosts. You never know, eh? Never know what's out there. Never know what could be watching you. Never know what —"

"You gonna give my twenty back?"

"You want me to tell you a secret, handsome?"

Charlie didn't answer.

She moved her face closer to his as if she were going to kiss him. "I'm not," she whispered very slowly, "a woman."

"What?"

"Only half, darling."

"What?"

She straightened. "It's Joe, right? Your name's Joe?"

"What?"

"That's your name, isn't it? Joe?"

"What?"

"Anybody ever call you Joey?"

"Joey?"

"*Joey*. Like the Joey on *Friends*. Chandler's roommate, you know? Anybody ever call you that?"

"No."

"Really?"

"Yes."

"Strange," the person who called herself Martina Hingis said. She turned around and kept walking west along the sidewalk. Neither of us followed. The cheetah-patterned skirt became an orange blur in the cool September night.

*They all started making noises
around 7:00 p.m.*

"Marriage," said Nikolai as he attempted to pry a small chunk of French fry stuck between his two front teeth with the tip of his pinky fingernail. "Please. You know what happens when you have a wife? You know what happens, kids?"

Charlie wiped his index finger along the edge of the empty white plate in front of him, sopping up the grease. "What happens, Mr. Khernofsky?"

"Consideration."

"What?"

"Consideration," Nikolai repeated. Giving up on his teeth, he plopped his elbows on the counter. "You kids ever heard the word *consideration?*"

"Yeah, I heard that word bef —" Charlie began.

"Course not. You kids don't know nothing. Consideration, kids, this word, it means when you're having some fun with a woman — the good stuff, you know — before you start using your, ha, your member with her, you know, with her box, inside her box, you gotta ... you gotta lick there first. Her box. You lick it. That's what's called consideration."

"You mean it's when you stick your tongue up her —"

"Eh!" Nikolai pointed a finger at Charlie. "This is a family restaurant. Watch it with the mouth, kid. Holy mackerel!"

"But isn't that what you —"

"Just listen, kid. Capiche?"

"Capiche."

"And you kids, too. Capiche?"

"Capiche," Oleg and I said in unison.

"Good. Now listen. You ever seen a Greek woman before?"

"Yeah, I seen a —" Charlie began.

"Looks nice when she's young, eh? Some nice dark curly hair. Some nice big knockers. Big eyes. An angel, you know? A flower. But watch, after thirty years old, after she gets married, finished. Kaput. Forget it. Fat, smelly. Won't do nothing but eat and watch the television."

"And you gotta give her consideration, right?"

"Exactly! No good stuff. Nothing for you. Never anything but —"

"Eating her ..."

"Eh!" Nikolai raised a fist at Charlie. "What did I tell you? Enough already. Holy mackerel! Too smart, this kid. Knows everything."

"But you said —"

"You see," Nikolai said, turning to Oleg and me, "I don't think I have to worry about Farley over here."

"Charlie."

"Charlie over here doing something stupid like getting stuck with, you know, some smelly Greek. He's a smart kid. He understands about some things. But you and Jimmy, I don't know. I don't know about you two. Sometimes ... I don't know. You're stupid sometimes. Which reminds me, Oleg, how come you skipped your boxing on Thursday?"

"Had to help with the groceries."

"The groceries. Who'd you have to help with the groceries?"

"Sonia. Had to help carry —"

"Don't call your mother by her first name."

"What's the difference?"

"It's disrespect. And don't lie to your uncle, either. I went grocery shopping with your mother yesterday. How many times she go a week, eh? Once. What are you skipping boxing for?"

"I had to —"

"You were pissing your quarters away in front of a screen, no?"

"No, I was —"

"Please, Oleg. School, sure. You're like your brother. Not so smart with the school. Basketball, okay. Dinner, okay. The dentist, sure. My funeral, fine. Boxing, no. Don't skip boxing! Your coach, know what he says? Know what he says, Oleg? He says you were the quickest — how old are you now?"

"Thirteen."

"Yeah, he says you were the quickest thirteen-year-old he seen at Sully's Gym. How about that, eh? Not so bad."

"True," Charlie said, smacking Oleg on the back. "That ain't so bad. You could be the next world champion, buddy. The hell you slacking off for? You gotta work hard."

"You tell him, Farley."

Charlie stood up from his bar stool, made a microphone with his fist, and in a voice shockingly similar to the one that

announced fighters in Mike Tyson 2000, said, "Ladies and gen-
tlemen, boys and girls, please welcome to the ring the Russian-
born —"

"Ravager!" Nikolai hollered.

"The Russian-born Ravager! Canadian-raised —"

"Killer!"

"Yeah! Killer! Canadian-raised killer! Five-time heavyweight champion of the world, the most feared man on the
face of the Earth. Put your hands together for Oleg 'The King'
Kkkkkkkkhhhhhhhhheeeerrrrrnnnnofsky!"

Nikolai drummed his palms against the counter. "That's
what I'm talking about! Show us your stuff, champ! C'mon!"

Oleg jumped off his bar stool and started shuffling around
the plastic-covered tables, throwing quick left jabs, bouncing his
head back and forth.

"Atta, boy!" Nikolai cried. "Give him what's coming!"

"Knock him out, big man!" Charlie said.

"Dance, Oleg!" Nikolai roared. "Dance!"

Oleg stopped in front of the doorway, ducked two punches,
faked with his right, ducked again, then came back up with a
gigantic left hook, pivoting his whole body into the swing.

"Khernofsky's done it again!" Charlie yelled.

"He's unbeatable!" Nikolai said.

"Still the most feared man on the face of the Earth!" Charlie
said.

Following Nikolai's lead, we all began chanting, "Oleg!
Oleg! Oleg ..."

Oleg threw his hands into the air, dashed back to the counter, climbed on top as if it were a podium.

"Oleg! Oleg! Oleg ..."

He looked past us to the hordes of adoring fans, returned
smiles, winked at pretty girls.

"Khernofsky," Charlie interjected into our chorus, still using his commentator's voice, "the first ever homosexual boxer, has done it again with his killer left hook. He's an inspiration to fags all over the world. Especially Russian fags. I tell you, he's the toughest homo in —"

Oleg stomped his foot on the counter. "I'll break your jaw."

"Oh-oh," Charlie said into his microphone. "Looks like Khernofsky isn't through with just one fight. He wants more bloodshed. This fudge-packer, I tell you, he just can't get enough —"

"Eh, eh, eh!" Nikolai clapped his hands three times. "Farley, don't be so smart. Oleg, get down from there. Enough of this. Both of you. This is a restaurant, eh? Down, Oleg."

But instead of descending from the counter, Oleg picked up the empty white plate we'd been gobbling fries off five minutes earlier and held it above Charlie's head as if he were going to smash it to bits on his Padres cap.

"Eh!" Nikolai hollered, grabbing Oleg's ankle.

"Who you calling a homo?" Oleg hissed, glaring at Charlie.

"Sorry," Charlie said, shielding his face.

"*You're* the homo," Oleg said, referring to Charlie.

And then there was forty-five seconds of rebuttal.

Charlie: "Christ, I was joking."

Nikolai: "Get down from there, Oleg!"

Oleg: "*You're* the homo."

Nikolai: "Enough already!"

Oleg: "*You're* the homo."

Nikolai: "Nobody's a homo."

Oleg: "Charlie's a homo."

Nikolai: "Are you a homo, Farley?"

Charlie: "I'm not a homo."

Nikolai: "Farley's not a homo."

Charlie: "Charlie."

Nikolai: "Charlie's not a homo."

Oleg: "I'm gonna break your jaw, you homo."

Nikolai: "Put it down, Oleg!"

Charlie: "I'm not a homo, Oleg."

Oleg: "Who you calling a homo then?"

Charlie: "I was joking, Oleg. I don't actually think you're a homo."

Oleg: "You're the homo."

Charlie: "I'm not a homo."

Nikolai: "Nobody's a homo already!"

Charlie: "I think Jim's a homo."

Me: "I'm not a homo."

Charlie: "Sure you are."

Me: "I'm not."

Nikolai: "Jimmy's not a homo."

Charlie: "Jim's a homo. Look at him. He's a homo."

Nikolai: "I've known Jimmy since he was a kid. He's no homo."

Charlie: "I bet you he's a homo."

Nikolai: "Put the plate down, Oleg!"

Charlie: "You think Jim's a homo, Oleg?"

Oleg: "You're the homo!"

Charlie: "Man, oh, man."

Nikolai: "Enough already!"

Oleg: "I should smash his face in!"

Nikolai: "Oleg!"

Charlie: "I was joking, Oleg. Calm down."

Oleg: "You're the biggest homo I ever saw!"

Nikolai: "He was joking, Oleg."

Charlie: "Bigger than Jim?"

Oleg: "Bigger than anybody."

Charlie: "So you *do* think Jim's a homo?"

Oleg: "You're both homos."

Me: "I'm not a homo, Oleg."

Charlie: "How come you're friends with two homos then?"

Nikolai: "Give me the plate, Oleg!"

Oleg: "I'm not even your friend."

Charlie: "'Cause I'm a homo?"

Nikolai: "Oleg, give me the plate!"

Oleg: "No, 'cause you're a —"

Charlie: "So you'd be friends with me if I was a homo?"

Oleg: "I don't know."

Charlie: "You faggot."

Luckily, instead of breaking the plate over Charlie's head, Oleg — it seemed he was in such a state that he needed to do something destructive in order to prevent himself from biting his own arm off — flung the plate across the restaurant like a Frisbee. It shattered against the far wall.

For a brief moment there was silence, then Nikolai shouted, "What the ... you ... you fool! Get off my counter, you fool! Get off! Get off, you fool!"

Slowly, Oleg crouched on his knees and slid off the counter.

Nikolai grabbed his wrist and pulled him close. "What's wrong with you, eh?"

Oleg didn't answer, stared at his shoes.

"This is a business," Nikolai barked, slapping his nephew hard across the cheek.

Oleg's head, like elastic, swung to the side and back.

"What do you think when you do something like this, eh? Huh? What do you think, Oleg?"

Oleg didn't say.

"You're lucky I don't tell your mother you act like this. Or your brother, Oleg. If I told Yuri ..."

"She always wear that black scarf on her head?" I asked.

"Yes," Charlie said.

"Even in the summer?"

"Yes."

"She doesn't get hot?"

"Shut up, Jim."

Charlie lived with his mother on the second and third floor of a blue semi-detached brick house about twenty minutes south of Oleg's and my neighbourhood. Save for the colour, his place looked the same as all the other skinny pointy-roofed porchless houses on the street with small balconies and black-fenced front yards.

Mostly Portuguese families lived on the block. His next-door neighbours were Portuguese: the Cruzes on the right, Silvas on the left. The two houses directly across the street were Portuguese: the Ferreiras and the Gomezes. And Charlie's landlord, Amelia Nunez — widowed, shrunken, prune-faced, moustached — was also Portuguese. She lived alone on the floor below him.

"And you've never even seen her wear a white shirt?" I asked.

"No."

"A red one?"

"No! Black. She only wears black."

"Not once you've seen her wear a white shirt?"

"No, Jim."

Mrs. Nunez had rights to the front lawn of the house, and where a sheet of grass or garden might normally have been, she'd erected a full-colour plastic fountain in the mould of a crucified Christ, designed so that a steady flow of water trickled out of his punctured palms and into a small ceramic-bordered pond below. A cobblestone walkway led from the sidewalk to the front door. On the other side of the lawn there was a pine tree, cleanly trimmed into the shape of a pyramid.

Rarely did I ring Charlie's doorbell when Mrs. Nunez wasn't outside, sweeping the walkway or trimming the pine tree. She never said anything to me when I came by. Just looked my way, frowned, then went on with her business. Sweeping, trimming.

"Think she wears black underwear, too?"

"Probably, Jim."

"How old you think she is?"

"A million." Charlie closed the top door on his desk and opened the bottom one, continued rummaging around.

"She always have that fountain?"

"Yes."

"Where'd she buy it?"

"I don't know. Wal-Mart probably."

"They sell those at Wal-Mart?"

"Yes."

"Really?"

"Yes!"

"How much you think it costs?"

"Sixty bucks … eighty maybe."

"That much?"

"Yes."

"You could buy a lot for that."

"No, you couldn't."

"Sure you could."

"Shut up, Jim."

"What?"

"The hell did I put it?" Charlie muttered to himself, shut the bottom door on his desk, and opened another.

"You ever see her when she wasn't a widow."

"No."

"She have any kids?"

"I ain't seen any of them. But probably. All Portuguese people have kids."

"They do?"

"Yes."

"How come?"

"'Cause they wanna take over the world."

"Yeah?"

"Yes, Jim."

"You lived here your whole life?"

"Yeah. Thirteen years."

"And you've never seen her wear a red shirt?"

Charlie slammed the desk door shut, spun around on his black chair. "Fuck, Jim! You wanna know what her shit smells like, too? Enough goddamn questions —"

"Watch your mouth, Charles!" his mother hollered from beyond Charlie's bedroom door.

"Sorry, Ma!" Charlie yelled back. "Didn't know you were home."

"What difference does it make if I'm home?" She sounded as if she was in the kitchen, two rooms over.

"Sorry!" Charlie shouted.

"Don't be sorry. Just don't do it."

Charlie rolled his eyes. "Like she's never said fuck," he muttered, then got up from his chair and came over to me. We both stared out his bedroom window, which looked over the front lawn.

"You find it?" I asked.

Charlie held the tube of red food colouring in front of my eyes, between his thumb and forefinger. "The resurrection awaits," he said, stuffing the tube into his pocket.

Then a yellow Honda Civic hatchback with NO FEAR stencilled on its rear window slowed down and parked across the street. Two bearish guys with flat-brimmed baseball caps and baby-blue track suits got out of the car and waited on the sidewalk.

"Know what happened to my dad the other day?" Charlie asked, watching the two guys through his window.

"What?"

"He was coming home from this bar, right? And he parked his Porsche down the block and —"

"Your dad has a Porsche?"

Lucio Gomez, the youngest of the three sons in the Gomez family across the street, ran out the front door of his house and shook hands with the two guys hanging out on the sidewalk. After a few words, the three guys hopped into the Honda and zoomed down Charlie's street, blasting a catchy techno song with the phrase "I want to fuck you in the ass" repeated over and over in a twangy, synthesized male voice.

"Your dad has a Porsche?" I repeated.

"Nineteen seventy-two Carrera. Black."

"Really?"

"You could kick me in the nuts seven times if I'm lying. That guy's got dough like no tomorrow. Once he told me he spent four hundred bucks on a dinner for two."

"Four hundred?"

"That's right. Four zero zero. He was taking out this girl. Called her a sweet vixen. You know what that is, Jim?"

"An Indian?"

"No, you dumb fuck. It means a —"

Somebody was knocking on Charlie's bedroom door.

"Holy Christ," Charlie whispered.

"Charles?" his mother said.

"Yes, Ma?"

There was a pause.

"Would the two of you like some dinner?"

Charlie glanced at me. I shrugged.

"Sure, Ma."

"It'll be ready in five minutes."

"Sounds good, Ma. We'll be right out."

"And, Charles?"

"Yes, Ma?"

"If you think I can't hear your filthy mouth from outside your room, you are very mistaken. Be respectful."

"Looks good, Ma," Charlie said, referring to the three thick grizzly pork chops lying with edges overlapping on a white serving plate in the middle of the kitchen table. The kitchen, so spotless and organized, looked like a kitchen from the "after" result photo in an advertisement for Lysol or Arm & Hammer.

Wearing red-and-white bunny-rabbit-patterned oven mitts, Charlie's mother rushed from the stove and placed a green ceramic bowl brimming with mashed potatoes on the table. "Hope you like potatoes, Jim," she said, then rushed to the fridge and returned a moment later — barehanded now — holding a see-through plastic pitcher filled with what appeared to be grape juice. "Hope you like cranberry juice, Jim," she said, putting the pitcher on the table and sitting at the head, with Charlie to the right of her, me to the left.

With her wholesome Anglo-Saxon good looks — sharp, rosy features, Scotch brown shoulder-length hair — Charlie's mother could have been the poster woman for a diet cereal or a dating service. She was young, much younger than Oleg's mother or any of the mothers who walked their kids to and back from school on my street. I figured she was thirty-two years old.

"Well," she asked, stuffing the edge of her napkin into her dark blue V-necked blouse, "you boys hungry?"

"Could eat fifteen buffaloes," Charlie said.

"Good." She served me a pork chop.

"Thank you."

"You're welcome, Jim." She scooped some mashed potatoes onto my plate.

"Thank you."

"You're very welcome, Jim." She served Charlie, then herself. "Would you like some juice, Jim?"

"No, thank you."

Charlie grabbed the pitcher, poured himself a glass. "What, Jim, our juice ain't good enough for you?"

"Be nice, Charles," his mother said.

"*Holy.* I'm joking, Ma. Sometimes you have a hard time telling a joke from —"

"Just be nice, Charles. That's all I ask."

Charlie stuffed a forkful of mashed potatoes into his mouth. "I was being nice," he said, chewing. "I don't get much nicer than that."

"Don't speak with your mouth full."

"Christ."

"Don't say Christ at the dinner table."

"You just said it."

"Charlie!"

"What?"

She put her fork down, glared at him. "*Not* now."

"What not now?"

"Jesus, must you act like a six-year-old!"

"Jesus?" Charlie took a sip of juice. "So you're allowed to say Jesus, but I ain't allowed to say Christ. How about Jesus Christ? Could I say that at the dinner table, Ma? What are the laws around that one?"

She ignored him, picked up her fork and knife, and began chiselling her pork chop.

"If you ask me," Charlie continued, "it's all a bit —"

"*Nobody* was asking you."

"Well, if somebody *were* asking me, I'd say that it's —"

Her knife slipped, clanged against her plate. She closed her eyes. "Shut your mouth and eat your food, Charles, or you can leave the table."

Charlie glanced at his plate, began flattening his mashed potatoes with his fork. "Okay, Ma," he said quietly.

She breathed deeply through her nose, opened her eyes, and picked her knife up again.

"But technically, Ma, what you just said is impossible. Unless, I don't know, you wanna feed me intravenously, how am I supposed to eat with my mouth clo —"

"*Leave!*" She pointed at the door.

Charlie leaned back in his chair. "You really have no sense of humour, Ma. I'm just kidding with —"

"*Leave!*"

"Really, Ma?"

She was frozen.

"Fine," Charlie said. He got up from his chair, nearly knocking it over, and strode out of the kitchen. A few moments later I heard the front door slam shut.

"Sure you wouldn't like any juice, Jim?"

"Yes."

"Water?"

"Yes."

"You want some water?"

"No ... yes ... I mean, yes, I don't want any. No."

She was staring at her plate, flattening the mashed potatoes on it into a pancake with her fork — just as Charlie had been doing before.

"He was mine," she whispered.

The next day nobody answered the doorbell when Virginia Nunez, Amelia's younger sister, came by the house to pick up Amelia and drive her to church the way she did every Sunday morning. Concerned, Virginia walked onto the lawn and peered through the front window: her only sibling was staring straight at her from the other side of the glass, eyes locked open, pale and motionless on her brown-and-yellow-plaid plastic-covered armchair. Virginia followed Amelia's eyes. Then she fainted, nearly fracturing her skull on impact.

"It was a miracle," she said later that day, describing the incident to neighbours, wiping tears from her eyes. "His blood, it was … he was … it was a miracle."

Charlie was right. Amelia *did* have offspring. A son. Victor Nunez. And Victor was an ogre, a caveman. Bulky, tall. Black fur had sprouted, grown, and curled over itself on his neck, front and back, fingers, arms, knuckles, nostrils, wrists, the inside of his ears — pretty much everywhere on his body you could see. Except for the top of his head. There he was bald as a baboon's ass. A crescent-shaped scar swooped down from the middle of his skull to the corner of his brow.

"How you get that scar, Vic?" Charlie once asked.

"Some broad tried to chop my head in two." He spoke slowly in a deep monotone.

"Yeah?"

"With an axe."

"What for?"

"'Cause I wouldn't marry her. But I taught her a lesson."

"What you do, Vic?"

He chuckled. "Chopped *her* head in two."

"You did that?"

"C'mon, boss." Victor reached under his shirt, scratched his belly. "I look like a murderer?"

He owned a renovation company, "Victor's Dream Homes," and drove a white van with those three words painted in pink cursive bubble letters on the side. His cellphone number, 416-RENO-MAN, was painted in black lettering underneath, and PLUMBING, REPAIR, CARPENTRY, WIRING ... VICTOR CAN DO IT ALL!!! was below that.

After Amelia died of what was diagnosed as a heart attack, the house went to Victor. He moved in downstairs and continued to rent the second and third floor to Charlie and his mother. Contrary to Charlie's theory about Portuguese people, Victor didn't have any children. He did, however, have three girlfriends that we counted: Mole on Her Neck, Pink Leather Jacket, and Hairy Cheeks.

Externally, they had much in common.

They were all white. They all had bleached blond hair with brown or black roots showing. They were all chubby, big-breasted, thunder-thighed. They all smoked. They all chewed gum when they weren't smoking. They all applied dark eye shadow and bright red lipstick. They all wore dangly silver earrings and fake pearl necklaces. When they showed up at Victor's house, it was always around 6:00 p.m., and they all pushed open the black metal gate and pranced along the cobblestone walkway in the same perky, poodleish way, their bosoms shoved heavenward, necks tilted back. Then they rang Victor's stiff white doorbell and waited for an answer, arms crossed, one foot forward, with indignant scrunchy-nosed frowns as if there was always somebody in front of them who had just loudly farted.

Mole on Her Neck came on Mondays. Pink Leather Jacket came on Wednesdays. Hairy Cheeks came on Thursdays. They all started making noises around 7:00 p.m.

Mole on Her Neck groaned in throaty, drawn-out intervals that slowly got louder and louder, and after about a half-hour, for thirty or so seconds, she made a noise as if she were crying. Pink Leather Jacket sounded like a rubber ducky being squeezed over and over. She never made noise for more than ten minutes.

Hairy Cheeks said things. There were about ten words she especially liked. Sometimes she'd say them in a regular voice as if they were any other words. Sometimes she'd speak them with passion and conviction like in a political speech. Sometimes she'd scream them furiously, like in a heated argument. Sometimes she'd whimper them as if she was being tortured and the words were being forced out of her. Sometimes she'd repeat one of them like a chant. Sometimes she'd refer to herself as one of the words. Sometimes she'd say that one of the words was all she was and nothing more and she'd been that word her whole life and the only thing she'd ever really wanted was to be treated like that word. Sometimes she'd ask Victor if he'd please, please, call her that word, please, that she deserved to be called that word, please, please, please, please, please, *please*. And sometimes, in his growling baritone, Victor would call her that word. Tell her she was nothing more than that word. Tell her she never would be anything more than that word. Tell her that that word was all she was good for and that girls like her — girls who were nothing more than that word and who never would be anything more than that word — should be treated like that word and nothing more.

Charlie's bathroom was directly above Victor's bedroom. Most Monday, Wednesday, and Thursday evenings, Charlie and I used to sit inside — him on the toilet, me on the edge of the tub — and listen to the groaning, squeaking, or curse-word-bellowing coming from the floor below.

"Get in here, Jim."

"I miss anything good?"

"Nah. Hasn't even started talking about her cunt yet."

And always, on cue with the first groan or squeak or curse word, Charlie's mother would fire up her forest-green Hoover vacuum cleaner, a very loud model. Sometimes — most often on Thursdays when Hairy Cheeks was visiting — she'd vacuum for more than an hour.

But none of Victor's girlfriends stayed over.

Pink Leather Jacket left the earliest, normally around eight-thirty. Mole on Her Neck never stuck around later than ten. Hairy Cheeks was gone by midnight.

Charlie and I would watch closely from his bedroom window as the front door shut behind them.

Pink Leather Jacket spat her gum out onto Victor's lawn, then lit a cigarette. Mole on Her Neck carefully removed her gum from her mouth with thumb and forefinger, wrapped it in foil, put it in her back pocket, then lit a cigarette. Hairy Cheeks lit a cigarette, still chewing her gum.

And they all strutted — high-assed, high-chinned, high-heeled — between the plastic crucifix fountain (still attracting a teary pilgrim every now and then despite conclusive evidence proving there wasn't a trace of real blood dripping from his palms) and the pyramid-shaped tree (which Victor maintained with the same vigour and discipline as his late mother), opened the black metal gate, let it swing shut, then turned north on the sidewalk toward College Street. Who knew? Who knew the sounds they'd been making?

That summer, after Charlie and I graduated from Lawson Street Junior High, and Oleg graduated from King Edward, and the three of us were en route to Dufferin Collegiate to begin grade nine, something miraculous happened. Charlie finally got one of their bras off. And you could tell Oleg was pissed by the way he kept rolling his eyes and grumbling to himself in Russian when it happened.

"She's not even that sexy," Oleg said, raising a hand in protest. "Look at her tits. They're too small."

Her tits weren't small. Each one was the size of a large grapefruit.

"And look," Oleg continued. "Her teeth are crooked. She needs a dentist. Look at her."

Her teeth were fine.

"She's ugly."

In addition to Oleg and me, there were five Korean kids crowded around Charlie by the time he had her sitting on top of a wooden desk in the front of the classroom, legs crossed, wearing nothing but frilly-edged baby-blue panties with a little red heart sewn to the crotch. "$E=mc^2$" had been scribbled, along with two other mathematical equations, on the chalkboard at the back of the room. Graphs and maps were stapled all over the walls. The teacher's desk was bare, save for a three-hole punch, two staplers, and a yellow mug filled with unsharpened pencils.

"And she's not gonna take them off, Charlie," Oleg went on. "There's no way. Not a chance. You'll never see her snatch. *Never.*"

Her chin was raised, and she was arching her back and pushing her breasts forward. She had long, straight black hair that dangled onto her bare shoulders. The plaid kilt she'd been wearing not too long ago lay undone and draped over a nearby chair along with the rest of her clothes. Pouting playfully, she waited in the corner of the screen for the next hand to be dealt.

"What you pick her for, anyway?" Oleg asked. "You shoulda picked that other girl, the blond one. The one in the wedding dress."

"Shut up, Oleg."

"You shut up."

Her name was Marlene Williams, a mulatto high-school senior whose hobbies included track and field, cheerleading, baking brownies, and having naked slumber parties with her girlfriends. To get down to just her panties, Charlie first had to remove her vest, shirt, tie, stockings, kilt, garter belt, high heels (each high heel counted as a separate item), and bra. The rules of the game were such that every time you lost a hand, your challenger put back on an article of clothing. And every five minutes or so you had to feed another quarter into the machine in order to continue playing.

Charlie — he'd made ten bucks earlier that day helping Lucio Gomez clean his father's van — had been sitting in front of the mini-arcade box for more than two hours and had probably drained nearly all of his pay.

"Watch. It's a joke. You'll lose three hands in a row. It's not gonna happen. They're gonna rip you off. You'll never —"

"Will you shut up, Oleg?" Charlie snapped. "Christ, it's not my fault you're a retard and you don't know how to play cards properly."

"I'm a retard?"

"You're the dumbest kid I know. How much time you spent playing this game? How much money you —"

"But it's true," interrupted one of the Korean kids. His bangs were dyed bright red, he was dressed in an orange-and-white Adidas track suit, and for some reason he looked as if he was wearing lipstick. "You couldn't do it, man. You won't do it. Nobody could. It's a scam."

"Shut up," Charlie said.

"It's true," the Korean kid repeated.

Oleg cracked his knuckles. "I'm the dumbest kid you know? I'll beat your face, Charlie."

"Oh, shut up."

"He tells me to shut up. Who is this guy? I should beat his face."

"Do it," Charlie taunted.

"You want me to beat your face, Charlie?"

"Yes, Oleg, I want you to beat my face. *Beat my face*? What does that even mean, Oleg? Maybe if you learn how to speak English —"

"It's a tease," said the Korean kid. "They just tease you. You'll never get her undies off, man. No way. No way, man. You can't do it. They make you think you can, but then you can't. Nobody ever got her undies off. You won't do it."

"*Undies*?" Charlie looked up at the Korean. "Did you just say —"

But the computer dealt Charlie his hand, seizing everybody's attention. His cards: jack of spades, four of hearts, five of spades, seven of hearts, two of clubs.

Charlie scratched his chin.

"See?" said the Korean kid. "They never let you win. Not once. No way. What are you gonna do with that? Nothing. You can't do —"

"Shut up," Charlie growled, pressing his finger against the screen to throw away everything except the jack. Four new cards appeared: ace of diamonds, five of hearts, seven of spades, ten of hearts.

"Shoulda kept the seven."

"Thanks for pointing that out, Jim," Charlie said.

"No problem."

Charlie held on to the ace and jack. This was the last deal: five of clubs, six of diamonds, jack of clubs. Charlie's two jacks started flashing, indicating a pair.

"Bet you she has a royal flush," said the Korean kid.

"Probably four of a kind," said Oleg.

"Shut up," said Charlie.

Marlene revealed her hand: six of hearts, two of spades, king of diamonds, ace of clubs, six of spades. The sixes were her only cards of value. They didn't beat Charlie's jacks.

For a moment everybody watching the game was quiet, waiting for a catch. Then, taking us all by surprise, $$YOU WIN$$ started blinking in glitzy gold letters in the centre of the screen.

Charlie stood up from his chair and tossed his hands into the air as if he'd just scored a goal. "I'm the king of the world!" he hollered. "The king!" He turned to Oleg. "How do you like that, you son of a bitch? You stupid retard dumb Russki son of a bitch, how do you like that?"

Oleg scowled and muttered something under his breath but didn't look away from the arcade box.

The same picture of Marlene Williams that had been in the corner of the screen now took up the whole monitor. Very slowly, in jerky electronic movements, she got up from her desk, slapped her cheeks, shook her head, then began pulling her baby-blue underwear toward her ankles, shifting her weight from hip to hip with each revealing tug.

"She's the ugliest —" Oleg started to say.

"Shut up," Charlie snarled.

When she finished undressing, Marlene dangled her panties in front of the audience for a few moments. Then, as if it were a banana peel or a used candy wrapper, she dropped the skimpy garment on top of the kilt she'd been wearing at the start of the game. A different heart, now that she was fully nude, had replaced the red heart sewn to the crotch of her underwear. This heart was black, the same colour as her hair, and shaped, I presumed, with the precise manipulation of a razor.

"I'm the king of the world," Charlie said again, and the young woman waved goodbye, blew a kiss, then disappeared.

INSERT COIN began blinking in the bottom right-hand corner of the screen.

Sandwiches.

I was afraid to look up at the ceilings of the Pepto Bismol–coloured hallways in Dufferin Collegiate Secondary School because I was afraid that one of the buzzing fluorescent lights might come crashing onto my face and knock me unconscious so that I would be left helpless while a swarm of kids attacked my body.

I was afraid to look at the hall monitor, all four hundred pounds of him, because I was afraid he might grab my neck with one of his gigantic pasty hands, lift me from the ground, and take a bite out of my head.

I was afraid to look at male students because I was afraid they might think I was trying to start a fight with them or think I was gay and checking them out. In which case they'd probably want to start a fight with me. Or if they were gay they might smile at me in a suggestive way and tell their friends I was gay and their friends might tell their friends I was gay, and if all those people thought I was gay, I probably was gay, and if I was gay, that meant somebody who *wasn't* gay would definitely want to start a fight with me in the near future.

I was afraid to look at female students because I was afraid I'd be making them afraid by looking at them. I was also afraid that maybe they wouldn't be afraid if I looked at them. I was afraid one of them might stick her tongue out at me. I was afraid one of them might point her finger at me. I was afraid one of them might smile at me. I was afraid one of them might ask me what my name was. I was afraid one of them might — it was rumoured Angela Saunders had done this to a grade twelve student — silently lead me down to a dark corner in the basement, turn her back to me, flip up the tail end of her skirt, revealing her commando preference, and demand insertion. I was afraid to look at the older girls because I was afraid they might slap me in the face or kick me in the groin or pull a shovel out from inside their bra and slam me over the head with it.

"What you looking at, boy?" a stout, shiny-skinned black girl with big hoop earrings and a tight beige skirt cut so short you could see the edges of her gargantuan ass cheeks barked at me in the hallway on my second day of grade nine.

Had I been looking? At her fat rubbery lips? Her bulging Coca-Cola-coloured thighs? Charlie told me black girls had fluorescent pink pussies and could make them vibrate at will, and if you licked them, they tasted like fruit punch mixed with cherry soda and milk chocolate.

"Huh, boy? What you looking at?"

I continued quickly on my way to the northwest corner of the third floor, entered science class, sat two rows from the front, and before I had time to take a pencil out of my bag, the kid next to me leaned toward my desk and whispered, "I think she'd let me do her."

Who was this guy? He looked like a teenage version of Danny DeVito — except anorexic.

"Bet you she just lets guys do her. Bet you if I asked she'd let me do her."

Charlie and Oleg had different periods, so I didn't know anybody in this class. I'd never said a word to this kid in my life.

"You don't think she'd let me do her?"

"Who?"

"The teacher."

"The teacher?"

"She's one of those types," the kid said, nodding rapidly. "That would just do it, you know. They don't care. They would just do it. Like if I asked."

"If you asked?"

"*Yeeuuup.* Like, if it was after class and I said, 'Hey, Mrs., how about we do a little fuck?' She'd probably just say yes. Doesn't really care, you know? She'd just do it for fun."

"Oh," I said.

"Or maybe I'd say something nice to her. Call her a nun or something."

"A nun?"

"*Yeeeuup.* Say she's precious like a nun."

"But —"

"And then I'd say, 'Hey, how about we do a little fuck?'"

"What the —"

"And then I'd say —"

"Both of you. Office."

Later I found out that Ms. Morgan normally taught gym class. Ours was her first year as a science teacher. Her position,

it was rumoured, had been appointed due to a shortage of quali-
fied science teachers available in our high school: she didn't have
the credentials, but phys. ed., the administration had figured,
was close enough.

Another rumour I later heard was that Ms. Morgan had
screwed the captain of the hockey team and the captain of the
basketball team and the captain of the rugby team and the captain of the football team and the goalie on the soccer team, all
respectively, in the third-floor janitor's closet. And, according
to Ronald Newman, with the hockey captain, Ms. Morgan had
incorporated his Bauer aluminum stick into the carnal act.

Rumours, rumours.

Ms. Morgan had the build of a Barbie: skinny, coned breasts,
tight cherry ass. She dressed like a Barbie: pink sweaters, tapered
white jeans, high-heeled sandals. She talked how I imagined
a Barbie would talk: quickly, in a high-pitched, giggly voice.
Her skin was the colour of an overripe mango, an effect that
could only have been achieved in a tanning salon. Her hair was
bleached blond, straight and long. Her nose, so small, sharp, and
dainty, seemed sculpted. Her lips: crimson, puffy, moist. Eyes:
fluttery, childish. Cheeks: hollow.

Really, our grade nine science teacher looked like something you might unwrap from a plastic package or blow up from
deflated rubber.

"*Now!*" Ms. Morgan bellowed.

The two of us exited the room in quick, long strides. As the
door swung shut behind us, I could see that our science teacher
had turned back to the periodic table of elements hanging over
the chalkboard at the front of the room. Like the first five minutes of the lesson, Ms. Morgan was standing, her back to the
class, tapping a finger against her temple and studying the chem-
ical properties with an expression that suggested utter confusion

as the students silently, now that she had made an example out of me and this other kid, waited for her to begin teaching.

"I'm Melvyn, by the way," my accomplice said once we were outside in the hallway. "Name's Melvyn. You got one?"

"Got what?"

"A name."

"Oh, Jim. I'm Jim."

"Jimbo-limbo," Melvyn rhymed, and I followed him — probably the only kid in grade nine who was shorter and skinnier than me — down two flights of stairs, across a long, straight hallway, through a glass door, and into the main office, where we sat next to each other on two of the six grey plastic chairs reserved for student offenders.

"Excuse me, Ms.," Melvyn asked the secretary, "you think I could —"

"No."

"But I really gotta —"

"No!"

"But I'm gonna —"

"*No!*"

There was no reading. No eating. No drinking. No talking. No whistling. No whispering. No laughing. No tapping. No doodling. No doing homework. No going to the bathroom. No going to the water fountain. No going to your locker. No wearing your hat. No listening to your Walkman. No listening to your Discman. *No, no, no, no, no.*

"But, Ms. —"

"I am not saying this again. *No!*"

All you could do was sit still and listen to the click of the grey Canon photocopy machine churn out paper after paper after paper after paper after paper after paper, along with the indecipherable low murmur of the secretary's voice talking into the grey receiver of her grey telephone. Which was sitting on her grey metal desk. Which was on top of a grey carpet. Which was surrounded by grey walls. Greyness everywhere. The ceilings were grey. The computers were grey. The chairs were grey. Even the secretary's face — droopy, loose-lipped, hound-doggish — was a mixture of yellow and grey. Her hair was white and grey. Most times when I saw her she was wearing a grey ankle-length dress with a grey-and-black-striped blouse. In the winter she wore a grey wool sweater. If she were to get a paper cut, I imagined that grey blood would drip from the wound.

Melvyn, feet dangling, fidgeting in his chair, sniffling his nose, scratching his little moustache, boldly decided to break the "no talking or even whispering unless it is an absolute emergency and that means a real emergency" rule.

"I gotta take a piss," he whispered to me from behind the sleeve of his white sweatshirt, which had an illustration on the chest of a chimpanzee bonking a fluorescent green elephant over the head with a gigantic sledgehammer.

"Oh."

"I'm gonna piss my pants. Know how much I drank for breakfast?"

"No."

"A two-litre bottle of Coke. One of those big bottles. Haven't pissed since then. It's all built up. All that Coke."

"You drink Coke for breakfast?"

"Man, I love the Coca-Cola. Drink that stuff every day. Breakfast, lunch, dinner. Doesn't matter. Love that stuff. Love the Coca-Cola."

"It's pretty good, I guess."

"You're telling me. Love that stuff. Coke — that stuff's the best. But, hey, what school you come from?"

"Lawson."

"Oh, I know that school. It's for retards and blind people and that kind of stuff, right?"

"No."

"Yeah, I know that. Just fooling around. It's a regular school, no?"

"Yes."

"Except it's for cripples, right?"

"No."

"I know that. Just doing some fooling."

"Oh."

"I came from St. Andrew's."

"The Catholic school?" St. Andrew's Catholic School was just around the corner from Dufferin Collegiate.

"*Yeeeuuuuppp.*"

"But isn't that a high school also?"

"*Yeeeuuuuppp.* Goes from kindergarten all the way up till the end. Till you graduate." Melvyn then told me he'd been kicked out of St. Andrew's Catholic School because the principal had caught him pissing on the side of the building during lunch hour. "I didn't think nobody would see me. They're crazy strict at that place. They'll kick you out in a second. For anything they want. They kicked this one kid out 'cause he swore too much."

"Yeah?"

"*Yeeeuuuuppp.* But you know my uncle — he owns a pool hall right across the street from here. It's called Pinozo's. Like my last name — Pinozo."

"Yeah?"

"*Yeeuuup.* You wanna come by there after school? They got a pinball machine, too. We could play for cheap. You'll come?"

"Sure."

"Yeah? But, hey, what you think the secretary'd do if I took my ding-dong-a-long-ding-dong-wonger out right here and started pissing on the carpet?"

"Dunno."

"Think she'd scream?"

"Maybe."

"Think she'd call the cops?"

"I don't know."

"Think she'd give me a fuck?"

"If you started pissing?"

"I'm gonna do it."

"You are?"

"*Yeeeuuuupppp*." Melvyn pretended to undo his fly. "Should I do it?"

"I don't know.

"I'm gonna do it."

"Really?"

"*Naaahhhhh*. Not today. Maybe some other time. But, hey, you know what's funny?"

"What?"

"*The Simpsons*. You like that show?"

"Sure."

"You ever seen the one where Homer —"

The secretary, wrapping a hand around her telephone receiver, glaring at us, stuck her neck forward and let out a loud and guttural I-am-going-to-call-the-vice-principal-if-you-do-not-shut-the-fuck-up-and-then-you-are-going-to-be-in-deep-shit "Ahem!"

"Ms., please, can I go to the bathroom, Ms.?" Melvyn asked, squishing his knees together.

She shook her head and continued speaking into the phone. Melvyn let out a gasp, and as soon as she wasn't looking, gave her the finger.

Flanked by Harry's Shoe Repair and Nickel and Dime Laundromat, on the south side of Bloor, one block east of Dufferin, across the street from Blockbuster Video, was a two-storey grey-brick building with an old sign above the front door that looked as if it might come tumbling down at any moment. PIN ZO'S PO L HA L ND CAFÉ, the sign read in cursive brown lettering overtop a peeling beige backdrop.

"Here we are," Melvyn said as he opened the front door. "My uncle — he owns this *whole* place. It's all his. All of it. *His, his, his, his, his.*"

"Yeah?"

"*Yeeuuup,*" Melvyn said. He stretched out his arms, showing off the establishment: a large, dusty room with small round tables and black metal chairs with no padding in the front; a pool table, a snooker table, a couple of more black metal chairs, and a pinball machine in the back.

There was also a long, varnished wooden counter that held an espresso machine, a fishbowl floored with small change, and a cash register.

The woman behind the counter, the only other person inside the place — a squat lady with rust-coloured skin and a wave of short, puffy black hair — raised her eyebrows at Melvyn. She seemed to be thinking, "Christ, not *again.*"

"Give me a set of pool balls," Melvyn said, strolling toward her. "I brought my new friend, Ethel. From my new school. Met him today. We're gonna shoot some pool, so give me some pool balls. Pool balls, please. Oh, and two Coca-Colas. Coca-Coca-Colas!"

"Wednesday, Melvyn," she whispered. "It is Wednesday. Your poppa will be here anytime now."

Melvyn squeezed his eyes shut, snapped his fingers. "*Shucks!*"
He turned to me. "I just forgot. I got ... karate class. I got karate
class today. My pops comes down and takes me to go to karate
class on Wednesdays."

"Karate?"

"*Yeeuuup.* I know all types of moves. Over three million moves.
My best one is the death grip. All I gotta do is push the right
place on your wrist and your face falls off. Then your arms turn
to blood. Then your brain explodes. Then it takes you three hours
and forty-two minutes and fifty-nine seconds to die. There's no
chance you could live. Want me to test it on you?"

"Okay."

"Tomorrow."

"Oh."

"I can't do it now, 'cause I gotta go wait outside for my pop.
He don't like to come inside. But, hey, you could stay here if you
want. You could play some pinball. Ethel, you could give my
buddy a free Coke, right?"

Ethel forced a nod.

"She's my second aunt," Melvyn said. "Or — whatchacallit?
— my step-aunt. She's my step-aunt. My uncle's second wife —
that's who you are, right, Ethel?"

"Yes," she said.

"My uncle's first wife died from the cancer,"Melvyn explained.
"My first aunt. That's why my poppa don't like to come in. He
thinks Ethel took her place too quick. Know what he calls her?
He calls her a replacement for a corpse. *Yeeuuup.* And plus she's
not Italian. *Nope, nope, nope, nope, nope.* That's why my grandmother don't like you, either, right, Ethel?"

She blushed.

"Where you from, Ethel? What's that place called?"

"Guyana," she whispered.

"*Yeeuuup*, that's the truth," Melvyn said. Then he rubbed his hands together, patted my shoulder three times, and strolled out the front door of Pinozo's Pool Hall and Café, whistling to the tune of "Pop Goes the Weasel."

I must have looked distraught because Ethel asked me if I was okay.

"What? Oh. Yes. Fine. I'm fine."

"You would like a Coke?"

"Me? No. I … it's okay … I'm not … I'm not thirsty."

She fetched a sponge from the sink, began wiping the counter. "Too much. He has too much energy, that boy."

"Melvyn?"

"Yes. Too much energy. He …" She stopped wiping, looked at me. "Your name?"

"Me?"

She laughed. "Yes, you."

"Jim."

"I am Ethel," she said, still smiling.

"Oh."

"You live close?"

"Yes."

"You like school?"

"Sure."

"It is good to go to school."

"Yes."

She stared at me for a moment, fiddling with her sponge, then said, "You could come back here, you know."

"What?"

"On Saturday. Come in on Saturday."

"Saturday?"

"Yes, Saturday."

She tossed her sponge back into the sink and began loading

the espresso machine for the small black man wearing a sea-green suit who had just walked into the place, sat down near the front window, and said, "Ethel, give me a latte!"

Saturdays were Schubert days for my father. This meant he sat in our living room in his navy blue nightgown and red slippers, ate plain yogurt, drank ginger tea, and listened to his favourite recording of his favourite piece of music over and over and over again: the 1942 recording of Schubert's Eighth Symphony ("Unfinished") in B minor, conducted by Bruno Walter, played by the New York Philharmonic.

When I was seven years old, my sister asked him why he liked the piece so much.

"Why *that* one, Daddy? Why are you always listening to *that* one?"

My father put an arm around her shoulder (the three of us were eating peanut-butter-and-jelly sandwiches for lunch on the steps of our front porch) and slowly whispered, "Because, Amanda, my dear, it's not long enough."

"But why do you like it then?"

"Because it's too short."

"But why do you *like it*?"

"Because ..."

"*Why*, Daddy?"

"Because it should go on longer, dear. But it doesn't. It's ... it stops much too soon. And that's ... you see, there's no ... there's no closure in this world. Nothing finishes."

"I don't understand."

"You never will."

My father's music gave me a funny feeling, so I normally spent my Saturdays away from the house. In the mornings I went to Nicky's Diner and ate breakfast (sausages, home fries, two eggs over easy, one thick tomato slice, white toast, and orange juice). Then — and this only started the second week of grade nine — I walked to Pinozo's Pool Hall and Café. There I ordered a ginger ale, sat by the front window, and watched Ethel tend to the afternoon rush (all men, all black, all speaking in a chattery foreign language), serving them coffees and lattes and espressos and teas and sandwiches.

Sandwiches.

They ordered sandwich after sandwich.

And Ethel could slice a kaiser in two, spread mayonnaise on one side, mustard on the other, stack three layers of smoked turkey, two slivers of provolone, a leaf of Romaine lettuce, four slices of tomato, drop some jalapeno peppers on top if you asked, close the bun, cut it in half, put a pickle on the plate, and place it on the front counter in less than a minute flat. Sometimes I half expected her to stand at attention and salute the customer after she put the sandwich in front of him. And often, as I sat watching her, this daydream started rolling that featured her as a soldier, camouflage-clad, crawling vigorously through a windy desert, stopping every now and then to fire her submachine gun at ant-sized figures scurrying back and forth across a distant dune.

"So how you today, Jim?"

"Fine."

"How school?"

"Pretty good."

That army nonsense would quickly vanish when the afternoon rush died down, and Ethel, choreless, came over to my table and took a seat on the chair next to me. She was so warm and timid up close. So warm.

She'd normally ask me questions for a minute or two, almost
whispering. "So how you today, Jim?"

"Fine."

"How school?"

"Pretty good."

"You don't skip?"

"No."

"Every day you go?"

"Yes."

"Melvyn skip?"

"No."

"Too much energy, that boy."

"I know."

"He get in trouble with the teachers?"

"No."

"You lie?"

"No."

"You sure?"

"Yes."

Then, when she seemed to run out of things to ask, I'd take
the ball in my hands and start throwing her questions. "How's
Raymond?"

"Watching his TV. All day he watches."

"What's he watch?"

"The soap dramas and the talk shows."

"Which ones?"

"The loud ones ... with everybody screaming and fighting
all the time."

"How come he watches those?"

"That's what he likes — to see people scream and fight on
the television for the whole day."

"What about in real life?"

"Real life?"

"He like to watch people fight in real life?"

"Oh, my goodness. No, no, Jim. Just likes to see it on the television."

"You like those shows?"

"No."

"How come?"

"I don't like it ... to see people fight."

Ethel, after I spent five or so minutes with her, had a way of squeezing my hand or petting my wrist or absently removing specks of linen from my shirt as she spoke.

One Saturday, in late November, I asked Ethel how old she was the first time she met Raymond.

"You mean my age?"

"Yes."

She stared at my ginger ale can for a moment, chewing her lip. Then she glanced up at me, smiled in her warm way, and said, "I was thirty-three, Jim. And I lived with my sister. And I was a cashier. I was working as a cashier at the IGA."

"Raymond was a customer?"

"Oh, no. His brother — Raymond's brother — was seeing a woman I worked with. A big woman. Very big and ugly. We all four went out together. To a restaurant."

"Which one?"

"Which what?"

"Restaurant."

"Oh, my goodness, you ask too many questions, Jim! I don't remember. But it was spaghetti. Italian. And I met Raymond and ... he was a nice man. He was old. He wore a nice fedora. He was dressed nice. The whole time, the whole dinner, he talked about his mortgage and his dog. He seemed very sad. I liked him."

"Yeah?"

"He was a nice man."

And a week after their spaghetti dinner, Ethel told me, Raymond called her up and invited her out for another. Three months later they were married. Raymond was seventeen years her senior. He already had two grown-up children from a previous marriage and didn't want any more. Pinocchio, his faithful German shepherd, was enough.

"You like Pinocchio?" I asked.

Ethel smiled wide. "Oh, yes, of course. He is a very nice dog. He don't bite. But my sisters, oh, my goodness, they are all so scared of him! They think he is a wolf. They think he will tear their heads off. But he is a nice dog. He don't bite nobody."

"How many sisters you got?"

"Seven."

"They all live in Toronto?"

"My youngest sister, she still lives on the reserve."

"The reserve?"

"The Arawak reserve in Guyana. Where I grew up."

"You're an Indian?"

"An Anglican."

"Oh."

"I went to Anglican school. That's what I learned. Nobody spoke Arawak. But Raymond, he is Catholic."

"What about Pinocchio?"

"What do you mean?"

"Is he Anglican?"

Ethel rolled her eyes. "Oh, my goodness."

"You take Pinocchio to church with you?" I persisted.

"You can't take a dog to church, Jim."

"You can't?"

"Oh, my goodness."

Sunday was the only day Ethel didn't work. Church, she said, was the highlight of her week. She never missed a service. Was an active member of her Anglican congregation. Sang in the choir. Cooked for the bake sales. Helped put up Christmas and Easter decorations. The fishbowl on the front counter of Pinozo's Pool Hall and Café received donations for her church, which she handed over every two weeks.

Two Saturdays before Christmas break, after staring silently at my table for a few moments, as if she were in some sort of daze, Ethel said, "He can't do it."

"Do what?"

"He don't like to no more. He never liked to much. He wasn't … he didn't like those things much. But now, never. Just wants to go to sleep."

"Oh."

"Not even a kiss. One kiss is too much for Raymond."

"Oh."

"And you know Melvyn?"

"What?"

"At his last school they caught him in the bathroom."

"The bathroom?"

"That's how come they kicked him out. He was playing with his …"

"Oh," I said.

"He don't go to karate class."

"No?"

"He goes to see the doctor. For therapy. Because he has too much energy … down there."

"Oh."

"Too much energy, that boy. He —" Suddenly, as if she'd just realized she had been speaking out loud, beet-red, Ethel scurried away from my table and didn't even glance my way once for the rest of the afternoon.

The next Saturday, Ethel wasn't at Pinozo's. Raymond — he was a short, lumpy old man with floppy ears and a yarmulke-sized bald spot — was covering her shift.

He walked to the table where I had sat down, put his hands on the table, and asked, "You looking for my wife?"

"What?"

"You looking for Ethel?"

"What?"

"What's your name?"

"My name?"

He leaned his head close to mine. "Yes, what's your name?"

"Oh, Jim. I'm Jim."

"Jim. So it's you. My wife told me about you. You bother her, eh? She tells me you bother her. Every week."

"What?"

"She tells me you bother her. Leave." He pointed at the front door. "Get out!"

I stared at him.

"Get out," he repeated.

I obeyed.

Then I headed toward Oleg's apartment, cutting through the alleyway. My sneakers quickly got drenched in brown December slush. That was the last time I went to Pinozo's Pool Hall and Café.

Alack, alack, alack …

The walk from Pinozo's Pool Hall and Café to Oleg's apartment took about five minutes. I always used the back door to enter. It was next to a dented NO PARKING sign. The NO PARKING was dented because Oleg used it as a target to practise his basketball moves. He'd been doing that ever since he'd immigrated to Toronto from Tula, Russia, with his mother and older brother when he was seven years old in 1992.

You could hear the echo of his Spalding basketball slamming against the metal sign from my porch, which was just around the corner, and during grades four, five, and six, I used to walk by after school (Oleg and I went to different elementary schools) and get creamed in games of one-on-one. Normally, around 5:00 p.m., Nikolai stomped outside from his restaurant, apron flapping, and told Oleg that if he heard the ball hit the sign once more, he was going to take him by the ears, strap him to his cutting board, slice him up, throw him into the deep fryer, and make French fries out of him. Enough already. Capiche?

"Capiche," Oleg usually replied in a barely audible mumble, head hanging. With nothing really to say to each other, we'd stand around in the alleyway, kicking stones, grabbing at leaves, spitting, until Oleg said something like "Video games?" or "Sonic?" Then I'd follow him through the scratched-up steel door next to the entrance of Nicky's Diner, up one steep flight of stairs, and into his apartment, where I'd sit beside him on the sweaty fake leather couch in his living room and watch him play Sonic the Hedgehog on his Sega Genesis, a Christmas present he and his brother had received from Nikolai the first year they came to Canada.

There was only one controller. I never asked if I could play. Oleg never offered.

Sonia Khernofsky, Oleg's mother — a snouty, raccoon-like woman — worked seven days a week as a cleaning lady at the Four Seasons Hotel on Avenue Road, just north of Bloor. Her shifts regularly began at five in the morning and finished around six at night. Which meant she was up by four and in bed by eight. And after she went to bed Oleg wasn't to make a noise. He couldn't watch television or play his Sega Genesis because her bedroom was next door. If he dropped something on the floor or walked too heavily, he'd get yelled at. Sonia was a light sleeper and wanted the apartment to sound as if it were empty. And eventually — after waking her up again and again — Oleg figured the only way to achieve this effect was if the apartment *was* actually empty.

So when his mother went to bed, Oleg tiptoed downstairs, out his front door, and re-entered the building through the smudgy fiberglass door that led into Nicky's Diner. There he'd spend his evenings swerving back and forth on one of the blue-topped bar stools, eating French fries and watching TSN on the mounted television set in the corner of the room.

Or in the summer, when it stayed light past nine, Oleg sometimes came by Concord Avenue, the tree-lined residential street around the corner where I lived, and the two of us would play road hockey until it was too dark to see the ball. He was Sergei Fedorov. I was Doug Gilmour.

Oleg's father, as far as I knew, was completely out of the picture. He didn't come with the family to Canada. The only time I heard anything about the man (mind you, I couldn't understand Russian) was when Nikolai told me — I was keeping him company while he closed up the restaurant on an arctic February night — that once, back in Tula, Sonia was about to get into her car when she noticed her husband screwing their next-door neighbour's fifteen-year-old daughter in the back seat. When Sonia wouldn't stop screaming and wailing and threatening to call the police, Oleg's father, who had by now pulled his trousers back up, put her in the hospital for two weeks with the handle of the car door, which he had first ripped off the car before using as a weapon.

"Some people, Jimmy, they have the devil in them," Nikolai told me. "Blind ... they go blind, eh? All they can see is red."

"Red?"

"Red. Rage. Sure, they need it. Like ... like food."

"Oh."

"It is true, Jimmy." Nikolai frowned, lifted the fold-out sign kept in front of his restaurant during open hours (I'd taken it in about five minutes earlier), and propped it against the fridge full of soft drinks and Fruitopia juices behind him. He took a step back, crossed his arms, and shook his head at the sign, which read: ALL DAY BREAKFAST SPECIAL $3.95. And under that, in small black print, BREAKFAST SPECIAL ONLY SERVED BETWEEN 7:00 A.M. AND 11:00 A.M.

I left my sopping wet sneakers in the foyer and walked up to Oleg's apartment. Yuri, Oleg's older brother, seven years senior, gave me his regular greeting. "Hey, it's Jim the bum-fucking cock-eater."

"Hi."

"Go get out of here and put your training wheels back on your bicycle and fuck your sister's bum."

"What?"

"Shut up, bum-fucking cock-eater."

"Oh."

Then, disregarding my presence, Yuri took a sip from his bottle of Lucky Lager and got back to the game of cards he was playing in the kitchen with two of his buddies from Lorenzo's Garage, where he'd been working since he was sixteen.

Oleg, sunk into his living-room couch, was concentrating hard on a game of James Bond GoldenEye. (He'd upgraded to a Nintendo 64 from his Sega Genesis two years earlier.) A peeling white wall with an open entranceway was all that separated the living room from the kitchen. You could see and hear everything that was going on in either room.

I sat next to Oleg and said, "Yo."

"Yo," Oleg replied.

"This fruitcake pulls in with a busted headlight," Yuri was saying to his buddies. "A black Beamer. Ninety-seven, I think. Chrome rims. You seen that car pull in, Leo?"

"A Beamer?" one of Yuri's buddies, stocky, with a crewcut and a small doughy face, said. "No, I didn't see no —"

"Probably taking a dump." Yuri slapped a card on the kitchen table. "This guy, every time I go take a piss, guy's taking a dump. Faggot doesn't even work anymore. All he does is shit. And it stinks the whole place. I never smelled nothing so bad before. How can you dump so much, Leo? What do you eat for breakfast?"

"Yo, this guy's a liar. I see you on the toilet every day, Yuri. Always. I bet you he takes seventeen dumps a day. Permanent diarrhea. Yeah. I see this guy —"

"You watch me take dumps, Leo? What are you doing watching me take dumps? You like the smell? It gives you a boner, Leo? Next time I'm making sure the bathroom's locked. I don't want this guy coming in there. Probably he's filming me. Gonna put it on the Internet."

"Okay, Yuri, you lock it next time."

"I will."

"Good."

"What's this kid looking at, eh?" Yuri placed his cards face down on the table, grabbed his thigh. "This queer keeps looking at me."

His two friends chuckled. "Probably thinks you have nice eyes," one of them said.

"Maybe he wants to ask you on a date," said the other.

"Take you to the movies," added the first.

"Fuck you in the ass," said the other.

And they both watched, grinning, as Yuri got up from his chair and lumbered over to the couch where Oleg and I were sitting.

"What's the joke?" he demanded, bending so that his face was level with mine. "What's funny? What's the funny joke?"

Although the two brothers had the same feline eyes and bulldoggish nose, Oleg was much better-looking and more

physically graceful than Yuri. Yuri was tall, chubby, awkward.
He had a bowlegged stride. His arms hung to his knees. He had
a potbelly. He was starting to go bald. He slobbered when he
spoke. His cheeks were red and acne-scarred, and there was a
pimple on the left side of his chin that never went away. It was
always there. It got bigger, smaller, brighter, darker, puss-filled,
dried out, turned yellow, pink, purple, orange, brown, but never
disappeared. And that December afternoon the pimple looked
sore, infected, and was a mellow papaya-orange.

"What's the funny joke?" Yuri asked again, his face so close
to mine I could see that the pimple on his chin had two long
blond hairs growing out of one side. "What's the funny joke?"

"What?" I said.

"What's funny about me?"

"You?"

"Yeah. What's the joke?"

"What?"

He turned to Oleg. "Oleg, how come Jimmy likes my face
so much?"

Oleg ignored him, kept playing GoldenEye.

"Your friend a queer, Oleg?"

Oleg didn't answer.

"Maybe you're both queers, eh? Boyfriend and boyfriend."

"Get out of here," Oleg said, concentrating on his game.

"Get out of here," Yuri mimicked.

"C'mon, Yuri," Oleg said.

"Huh?"

"Go play cards."

"Go play cards?"

"*Yuri.*"

"Yuri, what?"

"Leave us alone."

Yuri casually walked to the television set, placed his beer bottle on top, then returned to his brother. "You screwed a girl yet, Oleg?"

Oleg didn't answer.

"No?"

Oleg remained silent.

"Huh, Oleg?"

Nothing.

"You still screw our vacuum cleaner instead?" Yuri turned to his buddies in the kitchen. "Last year I come home one day from work and my brother, this pervert, he's in the bathroom, and he has his dick ... his dick ... he's trying to screw the vacuum cleaner! He has his dick stuck in the vacuum cleaner!" The three gasped with laughter. "In the snout! On high power! His pants around his ankles, and the stupid faggot, he couldn't ... the stupid faggot ... he couldn't get it to turn off! He thought ... my brother thought he was going to have his dick sucked off! He was crying! Tears running down his cheeks! I had to go turn it off for him so that —"

"Shut up," Oleg hissed.

Yuri swung around and slapped his brother hard across the cheek. "What? What you say to me?"

"Nothing."

"I'll break your face in half," Yuri said, grabbing Oleg by his collar with two hands, pulling him up from the couch so they were standing face to face.

"Teach your brother a lesson, Oleg!" hollered one of the guys from the kitchen.

"Don't take shit from that giant!" cried the other.

"Oleg," said the first, "if you knock your brother out, I'll let you bang my sister!"

They broke down laughing.

"Give him a black eye and I'll let her suck you off!"

They were in hysterics.

"A hand job for a bloody nose!"

They pounded the table with glee.

Yuri tapped his cheek with two fingers. "You want Leo's sister, no? Or you'd rather stick your dick in a vacuum cleaner? You'd rather go play with —"

"Enough," Oleg said through his teeth.

Yuri chuckled. Then he drove his fist hard into Oleg's cheek. There was a dry clap. Oleg's body swung to the side, then fell.

"Get up, Oleg!" one of the guys from the kitchen said. "Don't let him knock you down like that! Get up! Don't take shit from that giant!"

Oleg slowly stood up, holding a hand over the side of his face where he'd been hit.

Yuri stared at him, indifferent. "You're not gonna fight back?"

Oleg raised a fist to punch, but, with ease, Yuri grabbed it, flung it away, and jabbed Oleg in the eye with his left. Oleg tottered backward but didn't fall over.

"Pussy," Yuri muttered, fetching his beer from the television set. "Did you think, Oleg, that's what a blow job feels like? A vacuum cleaner, eh? What else do you stick your dick in around here? The drain pipes? The VCR? You try to fuck the VCR, Oleg?"

Oleg didn't answer. He'd been staring at his brother with the same crazed look ever since Yuri had jabbed him in the eye.

"What, now you want to fight me?"

Oleg kept staring.

Grinning wide, Yuri grabbed Oleg's cheek with thumb and forefinger and, like a great aunt who hadn't seen her nephew since he was *this* big, dug his fingers deep, twisted the skin, then pinched. "Oh, my baby brother's angry because —"

Oleg yanked Yuri's hand from his cheek, and without a moment's hesitation cracked him clean in the nose with his right. Yuri stumbled backward, wobbled drunkenly back and forth for a brief moment, then fell ass-first onto the beige-carpeted floor, somehow managing to keep the beer bottle in his hand from making contact with the ground. His two friends got up from their chairs and howled.

"Ha-ha! The little fucker knocked you out, Yuri!"

"Made you look stupid!"

"Kid can punch like Roy Jones Junior!"

"Eh, Oleg, you can have her, my sister! She'll bang you for sure! She loves tough guys!"

"Run, Yuri! Run away before your baby brother knocks you another!"

"But I forgot to tell you, Oleg, my sister's a midget! And she got a nose the size of my foot! But, hey, she'll let you stick it in her —"

The beer bottle missed Oleg's head by a couple of inches and shattered against the wall behind him. Oleg ran toward the door, but Yuri, his nose bleeding from the blow, caught him by the neck of his shirt, threw him to the ground, and began kicking him in the ribs and the face with his socked feet, roaring in Russian all the while. Oleg lay in a fetal position. Suddenly, the two guys from the kitchen were pulling Yuri away. Yuri was trying to fight them off. He elbowed one of them in the chest before they dragged him far enough from Oleg's body so that his foot couldn't reach.

That Monday, Angela Saunders — I'd never before witnessed her say anything further to a kid in our grade than the required amount of words it took to borrow a pencil or an eraser — leaned over from her desk in the back of Mr. Glickman's history class and asked Oleg what happened to his face and if he was okay. Oleg glanced at her, opened his mouth to talk, then didn't speak. She frowned. A red dragon-shaped medallion hung from her silver necklace. She began fiddling with it, running it back and forth between two of her soft pastel fingers as she studied Oleg's black eye and the bruise on his cheek, looking concerned and full of sympathy, a compassionate nurse regarding an injured soldier.

"Your face," she said. "What happened?"

Oleg stared at her as if he wasn't quite sure she was real or a figment of his imagination. "My face?"

"You got in a fight?"

"No."

"What happened?"

"To what?"

"Your face."

"Oh, yeah, that. Fell … fell off my bike."

"No, you didn't."

"Yeah. Some car door opened on me and I fell. Smacked me right down."

"I don't believe you."

"What am I gonna lie for?"

"Because …" Angela let go of her necklace, placed her hand on the edge of Oleg's desk. "Because you're a liar."

And when Oleg didn't say anything and just looked at her small purple-fingernailed hand as if it were a bomb that might explode at any moment, she bit her lower lip, leaned closer to him, and placed her fingers on his wrist.

On his wrist. Oleg's wrist. Her fingers. Angela Saunders's fingers.

Angela Saunders, who kept a cardboard Starbucks coffee cup resting on her desk in the back of the class and seldom contributed more to any lesson than a high-pitched huff. Angela Saunders, who had soft blond hair and peacock eyes and pouty lips. Angela Saunders, who, as the story went (most of it according to Ronald Newman), lost her virginity at age thirteen in the public bathroom at Kingston Park to a twenty-two-year-old Jamaican crack dealer nicknamed President, then had to get an abortion, then went on birth control, then went sex-crazy and screwed more than twenty guys in two months, then had a lesbian affair with a thirty-year-old Polish stripper from a club downtown, then started dating the lead singer of a rock group called The Weather Channel, then broke up with him because she fell in love with a rapper called Messy Jesse, then broke up with him because she fell in love with some DJ whose stage name was Funky Fingers, then broke up with him because she just couldn't handle being in a relationship right now and needed some time to think and make her own decisions without somebody breathing down the back of her neck. And all this by the time she was fourteen. And those fingers, Angela Saunders's fingers, were on Oleg's wrist.

Angela. Saunders's. Fingers. On. Oleg's. Wrist.

Angela Saunders! Angela Saunders, who left behind a trail of scornful female whispers and gawking male eyes wherever she went! Angela Saunders, who had a tattoo of an Asian character on her left shoulder and a silver flip-out cellphone and smoked long Benson & Hedges cigarettes, click-clocking to the curb in her black high heels first thing each lunch period to light one up, her bubbly ass perking upward, pausing, then shifting to the side with every frisky little feminine step she took!

"Poor baby," she said, placing her full hand on his, then gently squeezing. With a lascivious grin, she added, "You should be more careful on your bike next time then."

"Yeah."

"Maybe you should wear a helmet or something?"

"A helmet?"

"It would look cute. You would look cute in a helmet."

"What?"

"You're cute," Angela said. Then calmly, as if what had just happened wasn't a big deal at all — *like what had just happened never actually happened* — she removed her hand from on top of Oleg's. She leaned back to her desk, sipped her coffee, fetched her cellphone from her glossy maroon handbag, checked for messages, huffed, put her cellphone back in her handbag, crossed her legs, huffed again, uncrossed her legs, patted her hair, crossed her legs the other way, then — and this was her normal in-class position — stared at the synthetic wood surface of her desk as if it were to blame for all the bad things that had ever occurred in her life.

Melvyn, who was sitting next to Oleg, whispered, "Why don't you give her a fuck?"

"Shut up," Oleg hissed.

"What, I bet you if you asked her right now she'd take you to the basement and —"

"Shut up!"

Charlie, who was sitting next to Melvyn, whispered, "She's only screwed one guy, eh?"

"Who told you that?" Melvyn asked.

"Figured out myself. Last night."

"Sure, buddy."

"Swear to God. But I had to break through to get in, you know. She started to bleed."

"What, she was on her period?"

"You're an idiot, Melvyn."

"What?"

"Forget it. But how come you're so skinny? What's wrong with you, Melvyn? You don't eat?"

"Screw you, fatso."

"Fatso?" Charlie patted his small belly. "This is muscle, buddy. Hundred percent. I got a six-pack underneath here."

"Righto, chubs."

"You don't believe me, Melvyn? This girl ... this girl from my old school ... she saw my bare stomach this one time in swim class, and know what she said?"

"What she say, lardy?"

"Said it was like rock, my chest. Like Schwarzenegger's. Just looking at it got her all wet. Told me she wanted to —"

The sound of Mr. Glickman's metre stick smacking against the chalkboard at the front of the room caught Charlie's attention. "Mr. Charles?" our grade nine history teacher said, stopping his lesson.

Charlie sat up straight. "Yes, Mr. Dick-Man?"

Giggles rippled throughout the desks.

Blushing, Mr. Glickman clasped his hands behind his back and began pacing up and down the front of the classroom, a prosecutor, seething, accusatory, preparing to question the guilty party. "Tell me, Mr. Charles, tell me, please, what you were informing your friend of just now that was of so much importance, that was so urgent, *so imperative*, that it couldn't wait until class was finished?" He stopped in his tracks, stuck his head forward.

"Sir, I was just asking Melvyn a question about the homewo —"

"Was it," Mr. Glickman boomed, "such vital information that you couldn't wait ten minutes, the remaining duration of this period, to voice it, Mr. Charles?"

"Well, thing is, it was kind of —"

"Was it, Mr. Charles," Mr. Glickman said, nearly yelling now, the defining moment of the case, revealing the true character of the accused, shocking the jury, "your intention, while speaking to your friend, to disrupt my ... *my* ... class? Were you attempting, Mr. Charles, to distract students from the lesson at hand in order to draw attention to yourself? Was that your intention, Mr. Charles?" Satisfied with his examination, Mr. Glickman bent forward and waited for a response, eyes wide, jaw clenched, chin raised.

"No, Mr. Dick-Man, I —"

"Yes!" Our history teacher slammed his metre stick against the chalkboard so hard I was surprised it didn't break in half. "Yes! Yes, you were, Mr. Charles! You wanted everyone to look at you ... *you* ... you and your —"

The spitball landed just underneath Mr. Glickman's left nostril. It looked like a booger had suddenly dropped from his nose. Oleg, grinning wide, crumpled the McDonald's straw he'd kept from his drink at lunch and tossed it behind his desk.

"My what, Mr. Dick-Man?" Charlie asked, his voice high-pitched, innocent. "Me and my what?"

Instead of becoming furious and drawing more attention to himself, Mr. Glickman pretended he hadn't been hit.

"My what, Teacher?"

"Your ... your disruptive attitude, Charles," he said, fixing his collar, ignoring the laughter. "Your ... your infantile games. Your childish desire to make a spectacle of yourself. Your ..." He paused, searching for words, nostrils flared and sweaty, wobbly cheeks flushed. "Your ..." His lips were quivering, wooden ruler pointing, spitball still sticking. "Your —"

"My what, Mr. Dick-Man?"

He exploded. "Enough! That's enough! I have absolutely no ... no tolerance for this type of disorderly behaviour in my classroom! Quiet! Quiet or you'll all have detention! All of you! Now ..." He regained his teacher's stance, standing straight at the front of the room, metre stick in one hand, chalk in the other. "Now back to the lesson. Remember to take notes because there's going to be a quiz on this at the end of the week. I want to hear your pencils moving. Now, Sir John A. —"

"Mr. Dick-Man, there's something on your —" Charlie began.

"*Sir John A. Macdonald*, the first elected prime minister of —"

Then I heard that familiar call resonate from some far-off place in the hallways. The sound of a jungle bird with a bright orange beak. That throaty, tropical "*Pe-Kaaaaaaaaaaaaaaa!*"

"Mr. Glickman," Charlie interrupted the lesson once again. "I just remembered that me and Jim got an appointment with the nurse 'cause there was this squirrel in the morning on the way to school that bit Jim on the finger and he started to bleed. So I took a look at it and got some of the blood on my hand, and we went down to see the nurse, but she was busy with some kid who was puking all over the place. She said the squirrel might have rabies 'cause normally squirrels never bite humans, and we could be infected. And if we were infected, that could be real dangerous, so it was real important we both go down to see her when she was free so she could give us a shot or something. She said for us to go down at one-thirty, and it's one-thirty right now, so we better go 'cause she told us not to be late 'cause she's real busy. So we gotta go."

Mr. Glickman acted as if there were a sharp object caught in his throat. He was unable to speak. We got up and left the classroom.

"*Pe-Kaaaaaaaaaaaaaaa!*" Lucio Gomez, Charlie's neighbour — three years our senior and a high-school dropout — squawked as he walked toward us from the end of the hallway.

("*Pe-Kaaaaaaaaaaaaaaa!*" was the code noise he used to beckon Charlie and me from class when he was breaking from his job at the Toys "R" Us in the Dufferin Mall.)

"What's happening, Lucio?" Charlie asked.

"Fifty bones," Lucio said, shaking both our hands. "Fifty bones, bro. Sold this remote-control car I swiped from work, this purple monster truck with bad-boy rims, for fifty bones yesterday. On the Internet. Fifty bones! You can sell anything on the Internet!"

"Yeah?" Charlie said.

"Swear on my ancestors' graves. On the Holy Spirit. On Britney Spears's snatch and her two tits. Swear to God. No joke. Can sell anything. They'll pay 'nuff cash. Can make 'nuff cash, bro. 'Nuff, I'm telling you. Check this shirt I copped at Foot Locker." Lucio pointed at the baby-blue North Carolina basketball jersey underneath his puffy winter jacket. "Trust me, with this shirt, you don't even know. The broads — I'll have to buy a tazer to keep the broads off."

"Okay, Lucio."

"What, you think you're bad Charlie? Look at you two." He shook his head at us in disgust. "You're slobs. Don't know how to dress properly. Don't even wear cologne. I'll buy you some Hugo Boss, then you'll see where it's at. A broad sniffs that — she can't resist. Swear to God. Swear on my brother's Civic. On Tie Domi's two fists. Hugo Boss, bro — a girl can't resist. Know where I went last night?"

"Where?" Charlie asked.

"The movies," Lucio said. "Caught that flick *Eight-Legged Freaks*. You seen that?"

"No."

"Those spiders, bro. I'm telling you, they attack like champs."

"Like champs?"

"I'm telling you. Took this broad with me. And swear to God, she had her head inside my shirt for half the movie. Scared like those spiders was for real. No joke. I went back to her place after the flick. Told me if I didn't come with her she was scared an eight-legger was gonna attack her in her bed. No joke. And when I went back to her place, girl takes me up to her room first thing. And listen, swear in God's name. On the Virgin Mary. On Jesus. On my cock. On my cock and balls together. Know what she says? She starts telling me about her family, and know what she says? Know what she calls her father?"

"What?"

"Calls her father an asshole bourgeois. Bourgeois? What's she speaking French for? Girl's afraid to say *bitch* in English when she's in front of me?"

"Lucio, I don't think that's what bourgeois —" Charlie began.

"She's not afraid to go buck wild when I nail her, I'll tell you that much. Nailed her seven times in one hour. Seven times, I'm telling you. Broad couldn't get enough. Soon as I'm finished, she wants to do it again. Bangs like an animal, too. Goes buck wild. Scratching my back like nothing. Like Wolverine, I'm telling you. No joke. And she wanted me to slap her. I told her, 'What you want me to hit you for?' She says, 'Just do it.' Like Nike. Just do it. So I slap her. Fuck, what do I care? I slapped her. So what? She goes buck wild. Know where she lives?"

"I gotta go," I said.

"What you mean, bro?" Lucio rustled my hair. "Let's get some KFC. Classic Chicken Sandwich and a Pepsi for two bones. I'll buy you one, boss."

"I got gym next," I said. "Can't be late."

Lucio shook his head as if I'd seriously betrayed him.

Charlie patted my shoulder. "I understand, Jim. I understand. But I'll see you for last period. With Insane Stinky Troll Woman."

"Git in 'ere, mite," Mr. Perches said with a stiff, jaw-clenched nod toward the inside of the boys' locker room. He was leaning against the open door, arms crossed, neck straight, dressed tidily in tight blue mesh shorts and a white T-shirt. "Almost light, mite."

"Wouldn't that make me earl —"

"Git!"

Mr. Perches was an Australian expatriate, middle-aged, blond, hot-tempered. It looked as if someone had sucked all the fluids from his body, leaving only veins and muscles bulging beneath his skin. He had a slim, grapefruit-pink face, and one long vein above his left eye, which quivered when he got fed up. The angrier he was the more the vein twitched.

"And change 'er up. Quick now. No time to play with your dingalings, mites! Jus' change 'er up."

Inside the locker room we had approximately three and a half minutes to take off our regular clothes and slip into shorts and T-shirts. A second later Mr. Perches would come barging in, waving his beeping yellow stopwatch in the air. "You see that? Three and thirty, mites! Time's up! Let's go, let's go!"

Once, he caught Ronald Newman sitting on the change-room bench with his eyes shut, chin slowly falling toward his chest as he attempted to salvage a few last moments of sleep before class began. "Upsy-daisy, mite!" Mr. Perches bellowed. Then he grabbed Ronald by his cheeks, almost lifting him from the ground, and told him sternly that if he couldn't learn how to wake up properly, he'd smack him so hard that he'd sleep forever.

"But that's abuse, Mr. Perches!" a student exclaimed.

Our gym teacher stuck a finger at the concerned teenager. "I'll show you abuse, mite!"

Instead of practising our layups and slap shots and home-run swings, Mr. Perches had us jogging around the gymnasium, tossing rugby footballs back and forth. According to him, this was an important part of perfecting the lateral. Which was a key element in the *gime* of rugby. Which was the most noble and manly and challenging *gime* on the face of the Earth. The only *gime* worth playing. "A real mite plays rugby," he'd tell us. "Rugby's a gime for real mites." And not until we had perfected basics like the lateral — which we never did — were we ready to move on from our training and actually play a real *gime* of rugby.

"We're not Aussies like you, Mr. Perches," a kid once complained. "How come we can't play a real sport?"

"Damn right yer not Aussies. Aussies don't whine like little girls."

"You didn't answer my question, Mr. Perches."

"Like to know what it feels like to get a hard boot in the arse, mite? Eh? How's 'bout ye answer that question, mite?"

Truth was sports and *gimes* didn't excite Mr. Perches. Discipline did. When we weren't running rugby drills, we were doing exercises: push-ups, sit-ups, crunches, leg lifts, jumping jacks, burpies. And laps. Laps were his favourite. He loved laps. *Lusted* for laps. There was something about forty or so students jogging in formation around a track, the order of it, the simplicity, that Mr. Perches couldn't resist. His eyes bulged and his mouth widened with a childlike anticipation every time he said, "Git on the track, mites, and give me five!" Which was often.

We started our gym period with five laps and we finished our gym period with five laps. In the middle of some periods we'd stop practising our laterals and run ten laps. Some periods all we'd do was run laps. Laps were Mr. Perches's most common punishment, too. You were late for class: ten laps after school. You talked back: fifteen laps at lunchtime. You didn't run fast enough or you cut corners during the laps in class: twenty laps tomorrow morning. *Laps, laps, laps.*

And that Monday afternoon in December, one week before Christmas break began, even though the temperature was below freezing, Mr. Perches herded his class outside onto the field in front of the school and made us run laps. He stood on the sidelines, bundled in his orange North Face parka. And, like always when we were running laps, he shouted at us, "Faster, mites, faster! What are you doing out there? Waxing your legs? Fixing your makeup? C'mon now! You run like little girls!"

There was, however — and thank God — an escape. A barbed wire fence nearly ten feet high surrounded the field we jogged on. In a far corner there was a hole cut through the bottom just big enough for one person to crawl through. When Mr. Perches wasn't looking — if he was caught up yelling at some kid for not tying his laces or dragging his feet or acting like a little girl — you could slip out the hole and escape into the alleyway. And since there were so many students in our class, he rarely noticed you were gone — unless later that day he caught you in the change room retrieving your school clothes, which would result in a week of running twenty laps before school.

Oleg was the only kid I really knew in my gym class (Charlie and Melvyn had gym during a different period). So, while Mr. Perches was busy tending to an injury ("Scared of a little blood, mite? Only little girls are scared of a little blood. Git back on the track!"), we snuck out the hole. From the alleyway we sprinted to Nicky's Diner. It took less than five minutes.

"What is this?" Nikolai asked, seeming secretly pleased there was somebody to keep him company for the next little while when Oleg and I sat on blue-topped bar stools, out of breath, shivering, still dressed in our gym clothes. "Look who it is. Look at this. What are you kids doing out of school, eh? What is this?"

"Teacher was sick," Oleg said. "Let us have the period off."

"This is the truth?" Nikolai asked.

"Swear to God."

"To God?"

"Yes."

"Good." Nikolai rubbed his hands together. "I will cook some French fries. Nice to have a break from school, eh? No good to sit there all day on some chair. Your back bucket — it will turn to stone. Like a ... like some statue. Who wants that, eh? Nobody. Zero. Course not. But wait, listen. You listening?"

"Yeah," Oleg said.

"You sure? This is very important."

"Yes!" we persisted.

"Okay, good. Now, listen, I saw the biggest knockers I ever saw for my whole life today. Never saw bigger. She walked in here, this flower, with some knockers like watermelons. And what did she order? French fries. And what did she ask me, this butterfly? She asks me about how I speak, my accent. Asks me where I come from. And what did I tell her? You turkeys know what I tell her?"

"What?" we both asked.

"You listening?"

"Yes!"

"I tell her I come from here." Nikolai pointed at his crotch. "From down here! Ha, ha! That's where I come from! I come from down here!"

We skipped English class, our next period, too. Sitting around with Nikolai beat listening to Ms. Lawrence read *A Midsummer's Night Dream* to a class full of disruptive kids: "'O grim look'd night.' Mischa and Gabe, save the chit-chat for lunchtime. 'O night with hue so black.' Teegan, how many times do I have to tell you? You're not allowed to do your makeup in class. 'O night which ever art when day is not.' Who threw that! I'm keeping my eye on you, Ted. 'O night, o night, alack, alack, alack …'"

I trudged back to Dufferin Collegiate alongside Oleg, slipped through the rear exit, retrieved my regular clothes from the boys' locker room, changed, then stomped up to the second floor, arriving outside French class just as Mrs. Henry was scurrying down the hallway, out of breath, desperately running her fingers through a chain of fifteen or so silver keys to unlock the door.

"*Je suis tellement désolé que je suis en retard,*" she panted. "*Zut, zut, zut. Je suis tellement désolé.*"

I was sure she was once a passionate young teacher, Mrs. Henry — determined, full of energy and ideals. But twenty-plus years working in the public high-school system had gotten under her skin, turned her cynical, dishevelled, bantering. Her nickname: Insane Stinky Troll Woman.

"I bet you her tits are covered in hair," Charlie once said.

"You think?" I asked.

"I bet you anything."

Mrs. Henry had short, chubby legs and arms and a balding head of black curly hair and a swollen red nose. She was no taller than four foot eight. Her feet were practically square. And her fingers looked like toes sticking out of her palms. And they never kept still. They were ceaselessly fidgeting or picking or tapping or scratching. Which made it hard, while sitting in her class, bored stiff, not to imagine they might all of a sudden begin to shake violently, uncontrollably, and Mrs. Henry would scream for us to phone the office because this was an emergency, *her fingers were going to explode.* But nobody would answer, all the students would just sit there like a bunch of dummies, and she'd fall to her knees, bury her head into her chest, and let out a long, ghastly moan as her fingers burst, spewing shards of flesh and blood into the shocked faces of the students in the front row.

"*M'sieur Jim!*"

"Yes, Mrs. Henry?"

"Pay attention."

"Sorry, Mrs. Henry."

"Now, M'sieur Jim, that you are awake, would you please conjugate *manger* into the past tense for the class?"

"Don't know how, Mrs. Henry."

"We spent all of last week learning about this, M'sieur Jim. You attended. Have my words simply floated right through that head of yours?"

"Yes, Mrs. Henry. I mean, no. No, they haven't."

"Then speak up, *m'sieur.*"

"I don't remember, Mrs. Henry."

"I find that hard to imagine. It is such a simple verb. There aren't any *special* rules or tricks that apply. Think hard, M'sieur Jim."

"Sorry."

"*Zut alors! Zut, zut, zut!* I try, but you kids, you just … you just do not *care*. How am I supposed to teach a bunch of couch potatoes? All those video games and television shows have made you stupid. *Zut!* If Super Mario spoke French, you would all probably be fluent by now. What is the use with you kids? What is the use? *Zut, zut …*"

At that moment, his pants hanging below his ass, shoelaces undone, slouched over, utterly unaware of the disruption he was causing, Ronald Newman waddled through the front door of the classroom and sluggishly made his way to the only vacant desk, his dollar-store earphones filling the room with a high-pitched treble.

"Newman, turn your music down!" the tubby Chinese kid sitting behind him hissed.

With the absence of his music, his attention now no longer shielded from the voice of the teacher, Ronald, a look of oblivion in his eyes, stared at the front of the room, his thin face relaxed, the small bundle of pubescent facial hair on his chin wet, a drop of saliva forming on his gaping mouth. "Mrs. Henry?"

"What, M'sieur Ronald?"

"Can I go to the bathroom?"

"No, Ronald."

"Mrs. Henry?"

"What, Ronald?"

"Can I get a drink?"

"No, Ronald."

"Mrs. Henry?"

"What, Ronald?"

"Uh …"

"What?"

"Oh, yeah, uh … could I, uh, go to the bathroom?"

"*Zut!* You already asked me that, Ronald."

"I did?"

"Yes, Ronald."

"Oh, uh … well, then could I go?"

"No, Ronald!"

"How come?"

"Because you arrived late, M'sieur Ronald, and I am sure in the ten minutes you weren't in class doing God knows what, you could have easily found the time to go to the bathroom. Now you are in class. You stay. You sit. You listen. You don't go to the bathroom. You don't get a drink. You *do not go anywhere* until class is finished, Ronald. That is it. *C'est fini.*"

"But —"

"Enough! *C'est fini!* I don't care. *Zut!* Be quiet. No more quest —"

"Mrs. Henry?"

"What, Charlie!"

"How do you say *bitch* in French?"

"Excuse me, Charlie?"

"I was just wondering, because my friend Lucio, he thinks *bourgeois* means —"

"*Zut!* Out! Go! *Vite!*"

"Fascist."

"What did you say, Charlie?"

"Glasses."

"What?"

"Glasses. I need new glasses."

"You don't wear glasses, Charlie."

"I know. My old ones broke. I need new ones. That's why I —"

"Out! Out! Out! *Zut!* Go! Now! Out!"

"Mrs. Henry?"

"Goddamn it, Ronald! No more questions. Goddamn it! *Zut alors*, for Christ! *Zut!* Goddamn, *zut!*"

"But, Mrs. —"

"*Zut!* Shut up, Ronald! Shut up! You're stupid, Ronald! You're an idiot! I don't know what's wrong with you, but there is definitely something wrong with you! Get out of my class! Go to the office! Follow Charlie to the office, Ronald! The office!"

Jim sounds too much like bum.

"That's it," Charlie said, fiddling with the knob on the combination lock in front of his locker. "I'm finished, Jim. Not coming back here. Never. No goddamn way I'm coming back. Finished."

"Really?"

"I ain't joking. I'm through."

"But there's only a month left."

"So what?"

"I don't know. You might as well —"

"I might as well stay in school for the last month of school? For what, Jim?"

"Dunno."

"Zactly. There's no point. It's not like I'm passing any of my courses. I ain't cut out for this shit. Tomorrow I'm not coming in. Finished. I'm finished." Charlie pulled at his lock. It wouldn't budge. Grumbling, he began adjusting the knob all over again. "And plus, Jim, I got better things to do than sit around in class like an idiot all day."

"Like what?"

"What better things do I have to do?"

"Yeah."

"You think school's the only way I could spend my time? I got a ton of things I could do."

"Like what?"

Charlie kicked his locker. "These locks are the most stupid retarded things invented in the world! Left, right, once around, left again, pass zero, halfway, around again, back and forth, left, right, fifty-two, forty-nine, seventy-six!" Charlie flung his lock against the locker. "Screw it! I don't even need my gym clothes, anyway." But he grabbed his lock and started all over again. "Fifty-two, forty-nine, seventy-six," he muttered, turning the silver knob back and forth.

"Maybe you got the numbers wrong?"

"Shut up."

"I'm just saying."

Charlie let go of the lock, looked at me. "Know what it is, Jim? Know what she did to me?"

"Who?"

"Worsnop. Mrs. Worsnop. Know what she did to me?"

"How would I know what —"

"These guidance counsellor meetings really piss me off."

"Get to miss class, don't you?"

"Yeah, but it's not worth sitting across from that old hag for a half-hour. 'What's up, Charlie?' She's always saying that. First

thing she says when I walk into her office. 'What's up, Charlie?'
Go to hell. Know what she did to me?"

"No, I don't know what —"

"She was going on about major decisions and choosing things
and the future and all this other junk, and I was really getting
sick of listening to her, so I get up from my chair — I figure I'm
just gonna get up and leave — but by mistake, instead of opening
the door that leads out of her office, I open up her closet. And
you know what was hanging in Mrs. Worsnop's closet, Jim?"

"What?"

"A leather whip and a leather mask and this short leather skirt
with a silver zipper up the front. Just hanging there. Swear to God."

"Really?"

"You could go down to her office and check right now. And
there was a big black dildo lying in there, too — the size of my
arm. Swear on my life."

"For real?"

"No."

"Oh."

"But I did actually open the closet by mistake," Charlie said,
"and Worsnop tells me to sit down and she's getting all huffy and
her nose is starting to sweat, and she's really starting to piss me off,
so I tell her, and these are my exact words, Jim — swear to God,
I'm not joking you — I tell her, 'Listen, you saggy old bitch, I don't
need any more of your advice or time ...' And I was really gonna go
off on her, you know, but before I could say anything more, she gets
up from her chair — I ain't joking — and winds up to smack me
in the face. I'm not joking, Jim. Really. She was standing above me
with an open palm. About to give me five across the eye. That's how
pissed she was that I called her a bitch to her face. I'd never seen a
teacher so mad before. She looked dangerous. She looked like —"

"Okay, but what happened?" I asked.

"What happened?"

"Yes."

"What happened was there was this goddamn stapler lying on her desk, and I picked it up and told her I'd staple her nostrils shut if she didn't put her hand down. Then I backed out the door, holding the stapler in front of me, just in case she attacked, like I was a cop or —"

"Wait. You told Mrs. Worsnop you were gonna staple her nostrils shut?"

"Not joking."

"Her nostrils?"

"Yes."

"Shut?"

"Yes."

"You said that to her face?"

"Yes."

"You said you were going to —"

"Yes, Jim! Christ! But, anyway, I figure she's probably gonna make up some lie and get me expelled, so I might as well save her the trouble and just leave."

"So you're dropping out?"

"Yes," Charlie said. He grabbed his combination lock and again started turning the knob. "I'm dropping out. Not coming back here. I'll get a job somewhere. Start making some money, you know. Start making some cash."

"Where you gonna work?"

"There's tons of places."

"Where?"

"You know sometimes when I talk to you, Jim, I feel like I'm being interrogated. You know that? I never met a kid who asks more questions."

"I'm just saying."

"What? What are you *just saying*?"

"Which job you gonna get?"

"None of your business."

"It's a secret job?"

"No. Just none of your business."

"Why?"

"Just shut up, will you?"

"What?"

"Shit!"

"What?"

"It's her."

"Who?"

"Boys!" a familiar wobbly female voice croaked.

"Fuck," Charlie muttered at the floor.

"*Charles!*"

Mrs. Worsnop, the school guidance counsellor, was standing in the middle of the hallway with her arms crossed, glaring at the two of us as if we'd been gang-beating a puppy dog.

"That … that *language*, Charles." She had on white New Balance sneakers and tapered white slacks and a baggy beige button-down shirt. And at that moment, for some reason, she bore a very strong resemblance to a giant mouse. She took a step toward Charlie. "I've been looking all over for you, Charles. I called your French class, but Mrs. Henry notified me that you weren't in attendance."

"Guess she was right," Charlie said.

"I guess so."

"*Guess so*," Charlie mimicked.

"We didn't finish our meeting this morning, Charles."

"I had other things to do."

"Like spend French class swearing and lollygagging in the hallway with your friend? You promised me, Charles, that you'd wait in the lobby until I got off the phone. And you didn't. What's up, Charles?"

Charlie grimaced.

"Tomorrow, Charles. I'd like to see you tomorrow morning fifteen minutes before first period. We've been making so much *progress*. These meetings are going so *well*. It would be a shame, a real shame, if you were to give up on them at this point. I would be very disappointed. And I think you'd regret it, too. So I'm expecting you in my office tomorrow morning, okay? We can continue the conversation we were having about, you know …" She arched her eyebrows, and in a gentle whisper said, "You know, low self-esteem and —"

"That won't be necessary, Mrs. Worsnop," Charlie butted in, his face red. "Because I ain't coming to school tomorrow."

"You're not?"

"That's right, Mrs. Worsnop."

"And why is that?"

"I'm finished."

"Finished? Finished with what, Charles?"

"With this. With school. I'm finished. Done."

"You are, are you?"

"That's right, Mrs. Worsnop. And all I need …" Charlie, yet again, began twisting the knob on his combination lock. "All I need are my gym clothes from my locker over here and then I'm gone."

"Gone?"

"Yup, gone."

"You know it's illegal for you to drop out of high school at your age."

"Don't care."

"And what, may I ask, are you going to do with yourself after you drop out?"

"No."

"Excuse me?"

"No, you may not ask."

"Oh, Charles! Don't be ridiculous. Enough of this. Enough fooling. I'll walk you to Mrs. Henry's class and I'll see you tomorrow morning in my office. Let's go."

"I told you."

"What did you tell me?"

"I'm gone." Charlie pounded his locker in a sudden burst of anger. "And I'd be gone a lot quicker if these stupid idiot moron locks would just open! You have to be a goddamn mathematician to work one of these stupid —"

"Charles! *Language!* That *language is not* —"

"Shut up!"

Mrs. Worsnop was stunned. "Did you just ... what did you ... what did you say to me, Charles?"

Charlie ignored her. He twisted the knob a few times more, lined it up with a number, and pulled. The lock released. "Finally," he said. Then he yanked open his locker, grabbed his shorts and T-shirt (the only two items inside), stuffed them in his knapsack, zipped his knapsack up, flung his knapsack over one shoulder, and — without saying a word to me or Mrs. Worsnop — took off toward the stairwell at the end of the hallway, hands jammed deep in his pockets.

"Charles," Mrs. Worsnop cried, "come back here!"

He kept going.

"Charles, I'm not joking!"

He didn't turn around.

"I'm going to call the hall monitor, Charles!"

"Call the fat fuck," Charlie said, but you could barely hear him because he was already pretty far away. "Guy's so fat it'll take him a half-hour just to waddle up the stairs and get here.

Call away, Mrs. Worsnop, call away …" He disappeared down the stairwell.

Mrs. Worsnop turned to me, squinted. "What … what are *you* doing out of class, anyway?"

"What?"

"You're not in class. Why aren't you in class?"

"Me?"

"Oh … oh, go back to class," she said, and I scuttled quickly away down the hall, happy to escape without any punishment.

Nikolai tried again, this time using a dishtowel underneath his hand for a better grip. Still, the lid wouldn't budge.

Defeated, he placed the jar of President's Choice home-style extra sour pickled cocktail onions back on the counter and tossed the dishtowel over his shoulder. "Superman," he said, shaking his head at the jar. "You have to be Superman to open this. Why do they give me this trouble, eh?"

"It's because —" Charlie began.

"Please. You need muscles like boulders. They should make this proper. You twist, you open. Capiche, kapoosh. Ding, dong. One, two. Something good. Proper. But they give me this trouble. Why?"

"It's cause you're —"

"Mountain muscles!" Nikolai made a fist at the jar. "You need mountain muscles to open this! They think I'm Nikolai the muscle builder with muscles like mountains? Eh? That's what they think? How come they don't make it regular?"

"It's 'cause you're not —"

"What? What is it, smartie pants?"

Charlie grinned. "It's 'cause you're not strong enough. I bet you I could open that no problem. Hand it over."

"You?"

"Hand it over."

"You who thinks you are so smart you don't have to go to school like the other kids? You think you have some muscles? You think you could open this?"

"Hand it over."

Oleg swung his bar stool toward Charlie. "You couldn't open nothing. You're a weakling. I bet even Jim could lift more than you."

"Ifyou'regaysaywhat," Charlie said.

Oleg frowned. "What?"

"Aha!" Charlie said. "It's true!"

"What?"

"And he admits it again."

"Fuck you."

"Forget it!" Nikolai grabbed the jar of pickled onions and placed it behind him on a wooden shelf. "Forget it. Who needs them? They're no good for … for the toilet. They give me the swamps, you know?"

"The what?" Charlie asked.

"The swamps. These onions. Who needs them? I eat one too many and then, kaput — two hours on the toilet. The swamps."

"The swamps?"

"The swamps. Sure. Swamp comes out, you know? Who needs that?"

"Swamp comes out of what?"

"The bucket. The back bucket."

"What?"

"The dump truck."

"*The dump truck?*"

"Sure. The pipes back there. Swamp comes out."

"What pipes?"

Nikolai shook his head at Charlie and stuck a finger at him. "Listen, Farley, you're a smart kid. Real smart. Not like Jimmy and Oleg over here. These two, I don't know. They're turkeys. But you know some things. Some smart things. So what is this business I hear about you?"

"What business?"

"What are you doing quitting school?"

"I was sick of —"

"Because if you think you are so smart you don't need any school, you better start making some dough, because if you don't, if you sit around all day like a bum, next thing you know, that's you."

"What's me?"

"A bum! You! A beggar. No home. Eating garbage from the street like the pigeons. You're smart — doesn't matter. You know some things — doesn't matter. You have some friends — forget it. If you don't do nothing, if you sit around all day — kaput. That's you. A bum. And who wants to eat garbage for breakfast?"

"Who said I wasn't gonna get a —"

"Like this bum at the station. Ossington subway station. This kid, what is he, seventeen years old? Every day I see him. Purple hair. The same raincoat he wears every day. What's he a bum for? Doesn't want to go to school? He can't get a job? Please. His whole life to live and still he mopes around every day like a pigeon, eating garbage. Please. You better get a job, Farley."

"I will."

"You have to work. If you don't work, you have nothing. You disappear."

"Disappear?"

"Sure. Disappear. Like … like a ghost. Some ghost. You forget you have a life."

"If you don't work?"

"Sure."

"What if you're a millionaire?"

"Still, you work."

"Why?"

"Please. You think you can lie on the beach all day? Every day for your life? Baloney. Forget it. You disappear. Every man must work."

"What if —"

"But if you have no money — kaput. You're finished. Done for. In the grave. What kind of woman with nice knockers and a good face — a good face with a good small nose — wants a man with nothing? Who can't buy her nothing?"

"Well, I know a couple of girls who —"

"Baloney! You have to buy a woman some nice things. Cutlery. Woman loves some nice cutlery. Good-quality cutlery. Silver. But if you have no money — kaput. No good stuff. Won't even take their shoes off."

"What about if —"

"Listen, what are you now, twelve, thirteen years old?"

"Fourteen," Charlie said.

"Fourteen? Holy mackerel! You're an old man, kid." Nikolai turned to his nephew. "And you, Oleg? How old are you?"

"Fourteen."

"Jimmy, what about you?"

"Fourteen."

"All of you? Fourteen?" Nikolai smacked his forehead. "You kids are a bunch of old men and still you sit around here like a bunch of kids! Please. Know what year I was born?"

"Sixteen twenty —" Charlie began.

"Forty-four. Nineteen forty-four. So when I was fourteen, that was ... which one of you knows math? What year is fourteen years later?"

"Fifty-eight," I said. "Nineteen fifty-eight."

"Fifty-eight, right. That was — Khrushchev came in that year. Khrushchev. You kids know who that is?"

"Who?" I asked.

"Khrushchev."

"Douche Head?" Charlie asked.

"Khrushchev! Khrushchev the locksmith who ruled the Soviet Union! You kids don't know a thing about nothing. And you, Oleg, this is where you come from."

"I thought I came from down —"

"Don't be a fool. Now. Let's see. Nineteen fifty-eight. Already I was a man. I had a beard. You kids don't even have a moustache yet. And how many years … five years! That was five years after Stalin went kaput. His brain — kaput. You kids don't know what happened at his funeral?"

"What?" Charlie said.

"You think Hitler was bad?"

"Yeah, well, he was pretty —"

"Baloney. Stalin, they showed his body for his funeral, his funeral at Red Square — Red Square in Moscow — and what happens? You kids know what happens?"

"Didn't he —" I began.

"Course not. You kids don't even know less than nothing. But listen. It was a stampede."

"What?" Charlie said.

"At the funeral. A stampede. Like … like in the jungle. Two hundred people, more, they trample each other so they could get a peek at Stalin's corpse! Hundreds dead! Even after he goes kaput, still he keeps it up!"

"You mean they —" I tried to say.

"But listen. Listen up." Nikolai motioned for the three of us to bring our heads closer to him. We obeyed. "This is important. Very important. You listening?"

"No, Nick, we're not —" Charlie started to say.

"Ketchup," he said.

"What?"

"How come they do it?"

"Do what?"

"This garbage. How come people put this garbage on my fries, eh? The best fries, the finest fries in Toronto, and then they put this garbage on them. These tomatoes. Jimmy?"

"Yeah?"

"How many years you been coming here?"

"Dunno. Six, seven years —"

"You ever put ketchup on the fries I serve you?"

"Maybe a of couple —"

"That's right! Jimmy don't put no ketchup on my fries! He knows what's good." Nikolai turned to Charlie. "He might not be so smart like you, eh? Not such a smartie pants. But at least he knows what's good. He knows to stay in school so he can get a good job, so he doesn't end up like no bum on the street and eat garbage for breakfast like the pigeons. And he knows what's already good so he doesn't have to put no ketchup on them. You have something good — what do you need extra for? Sometimes it's better to be … simple. It's smarter to be simple. Like a … like some box. A cardboard box. Simple. Easy. Sometimes it's better to act like that. Just a box. Right, Jimmy?"

"Sure."

"That's right, Jimmy! How long I know you, Jimmy?"

"Seven, eight —"

"That's right, kid! Ever since you was little. And tell me. One thing. One thing you must tell me. This is very important. Now listen. You ever tasted better fries than here, Jimmy?"

"I …"

"You ever go into a restaurant in this city and taste better fries than here, Jimmy?"

"I don't ..."

"Course not! If mine aren't the best in Toronto, kids, I'll chop my hands off with a butcher knife! Ha, ha! The both of them, one after the other!"

In late May, two weeks after Charlie dropped out of high school, my phone rang.

I was lying on my bed, watching a small spider spin a web in the corner of the ceiling and listening to the Blue Jays game on The Fan 590. The reception wasn't good. A shrill, buzzing noise accompanied Tom Cheek's play-by-play commentary.

The only person who ever called my house past 7:00 p.m. when my sister wasn't around — she'd graduated from Queen's University and was three and a half weeks into a solo month-long backpacking trip across Western Europe — was Charlie. So I picked up the receiver of the grey phone on my bedside table on the second ring, and in my deepest, raspiest voice, said, "House of Lords, God speaking."

"Who?"

"What?"

"Sorry, I must have the wrong number." And she hung up before I could say anything more.

When the phone rang ten seconds later, I answered in my regular voice. "Hello."

"Jim?"

"Yes?"

"Is Charlie there?"

"What?"

"Is Charlie there?"

"Who is this?"

"It's his mother."

"Whose mother?"

"Charlie's mother."

"Oh."

"Is he there?"

"Who?"

"Charlie."

"No."

"Do you know where he is?"

"Charlie?"

"Yes."

"No."

"You sure?"

"Yes."

"He's not at your place?"

"No."

"Why doesn't he just call me!"

"What?"

"He drops out of school and he's not at home when I get home from work and still he doesn't even call me to say where he is and he doesn't have a job and it's his own grave he's digging."

"Oh."

"He could be anywhere."

"Probably at the arcade."

"You know I can't sleep without the radio on, Jim? Can't stand it without the radio. Without somebody speaking."

"What?"

"And he might stay out all night. Might not even come home for the night, and he wouldn't even call to tell me where he is."

"Oh."

"If you see him, Jim, could you have him call me?"

"Yes."

"Promise?"

"Yes."

"Thank you, Jim. You're such a ... you're very kind. I'm sorry for bothering you. Good night, Jim."

"Good night."

Charlie was sitting with his legs outstretched on one of the orange swervy-bottomed plastic chairs in the front room of the Fun Village Arcade, smoking a cigarette and squinting at the soccer match playing on George's small television set.

I sat on the chair next to him. "Jays lost to Tampa Bay."

"Surprise, surprise."

"And Delgado could have tied it up in the eighth, but he flied to left field with two out and the bases loaded."

"He's shit."

George — he was leaning forward in his white lawn chair behind the counter with his fists in his cheeks and an unlit cigar butt sticking out the side of his mouth — had the soccer match turned up high, so you had to speak louder than normal to hear over the two frantic Italian commentators.

"And that puts them two games below five —"

"Who cares, Jim?" Charlie said, disregarding the soccer match and turning to me.

"Dunno. I —"

"They're shit. They suck."

"Yeah, but —"

"*Shit*, Jim. They're shit. But listen." Charlie took his Padres cap off, scratched his head, put the cap back on. "You know where I was today?"

"Where?"

"Victor paid me twenty bucks in the morning to help him move some furniture into his house."

"Yeah?"

"Yeah, and after that I went to 7-Eleven to buy some smokes and a microwave burger with the dough. And know who was in the place getting a Slurpee — a mega-size Slurpee, Mountain Dew flavour?"

"Who?"

"This girl I know from my old school. Simone. And we started talking. She's our age. Goes to Central Commerce. And she gave me her number. And I swear she was … you don't believe me, eh?"

"What?"

"I'm gonna call her tonight. Watch."

"I will."

"You'll see."

After a few moments, I said, "Your mom was looking for you."

"How you know?"

"She called my house."

"She did? What she say?"

"Said she was looking for you."

Charlie made his face into an old lady's. "'If you're not going to be in school, fine. It's your own grave you're digging and there's nothing I can do to stop you. But if you're just going to mope around all day and get into trouble, you can pack your bags and hit the road and —' Christ, she just has to relax."

"Think she'd actually kick you out?"

"If she did, I could always probably get my dad to let me move in with him or something like that. Or maybe he'd just pay for an apartment for me or something. Guy owns real estate all over the place."

"Yeah?"

"Course."

"Where?"

"All over the place."

"You mean he —"

At that moment somebody must have scored a goal because the soccer commentators burst into a howling chorus, repeating a word that sounded like "*Fugilianooooooo!*" over and over. George stood up from his chair and stuck his head close to the television screen to get a better look at the action.

"Italia win?" Charlie hollered.

George turned to Charlie, raised a finger at him, then broke down in a gasping, violent burst of laughter. He smacked the counter with an open palm and fell to his knees, disappearing from sight.

"Hell's so funny?" Charlie muttered as he walked over to the counter.

I followed. We both peered over the edge. George was lying on his back, his hands grasping his throat, laughing so hard that spit was dribbling out the side of his mouth and his face was turning red and …

"The fucker's choking!" Charlie shouted.

George looked up at us, shook his head rapidly up and down in a gesture that seemed to say, "Yes, you idiots, I *am* choking," and let out a faint, walrus-like croak, the only sound he now appeared capable of making.

"*Fugilianooooooo!*" roared the soccer announcers.

The only other people in the arcade were two Korean kids — both wearing white Exco track suits with black stripes down the sides, one with "#1" printed on the back, the other with "#2." They rushed over to the counter from the backroom.

Korean Kid Number One asked, "What's going on?"

"George's choking!" Charlie said.

"He's choking?"

"Look at him!"

Both Koreans glanced over the counter.

Korean Kid Number Two said, "He is choking!"

"I know!" Charlie said.

"Holy smokes!" said Korean Kid Number One.

"What should we do?" said Korean Kid Number Two.

"You know CPR?" Charlie asked.

"No," both Koreans said.

"An ambulance!" Charlie cried. "We gotta call an ambulance!"

"Where's the phone?" Korean Kid Number Two asked.

Charlie leaned far over the counter. "Where's your phone, George?"

George rolled onto his stomach, kicked the floor a few times, then rolled onto his back again, making no indication of where his phone might be.

"A pay phone!" Charlie turned to Korean Kid Number Two. "Go use a pay phone and call an ambulance!"

"Where's a pay phone around here?"

"There's a pay phone right around the corner!"

"Which corner?"

"You'll see it."

Korean Number Two hesitated. "I don't know where it is. You go."

"You're an idiot!" Charlie pushed him out of the way to get to the front door.

Korean Number Two pushed Charlie back.

Charlie swung around. "The hell's your problem, buddy?"

"Watch where you're going."

"Touch me again and I'll punch your teeth out."

"I got three cousins who live next door," Korean Number Two said. "Try anything and you'll be dead in a second."

"You have three cousins who live next door and still you don't know where the pay phone is that's right around the corner? What, you can't see out those little slits? Christ, you're a real —"

Korean Number Two shoved Charlie, who fell back a few feet. "*Fugilianoooooooo!*"

Charlie pushed Korean Number Two, who fell back a few feet. "*Fugilianoooooooo!*"

George began slamming his foot hard against the floor. Everybody forgot about fighting one another and ran back to the edge of the counter.

We all stared down at George. His cheeks filled with air. He bashed his foot so hard against the counter that the oven keeping beef patties warm wobbled back and forth. Then, suddenly, he was still. His hands loosened around his throat. His legs relaxed. He was limp. A rag doll. No sign of breath.

"Holy shit," Charlie whispered.

"Fuck," Korean Number One mumbled.

Korean Number Two muttered something in Korean.

"Holy shit," Charlie whispered again.

"*Fugilianoooooooo!*" yowled the television set. And, just like that, as if the voice of the Italian soccer commentator had performed a holy act of resurrection, George coughed and out popped a small brown chunk of something from his mouth, landing softly on his chest.

George slowly stood up. The chunk fell onto the floor. He stared at it for a few moments, then turned to us. "My cigar." Then he sat down on his white lawn chair, put his feet up on the counter, and, as if nearly choking to death was as much a part of his daily routine as taking a piss when he woke up in the morning, continued to watch the soccer game, his neck and collar still wet from the saliva that had been dribbling from his mouth a minute earlier.

"*Fugilianoooooooo!*"

The phone booth smelled like wet leaves and urine.

"How could that dumb Chink not know where this was?" Charlie picked up the receiver. "Right around the corner like I said. Hell's wrong with those kids?"

"Dunno."

"Know what I think, Jim?"

"What?"

"Incest."

"What?"

"Korea. In Korea they have the highest rate of incest in the whole world, right?"

"Really?" I said.

"You didn't know that? It's 'cause it's — whaddaya call it? — socially acceptable."

"What?"

"For brothers to screw their sisters — it's socially acceptable. An ancient tradition, part of their culture and all that. And I bet you the reason those kids are so stupid is 'cause they got brothers and sisters for parents."

"Sure."

"It's true, Jim. Swear on my life, that's the reason. I'll bet you fifty bucks."

"You don't have fifty bucks."

"Sure I do."

"How'd you get fifty bucks?"

"None of your business."

"It's none of my business?"

"Yes."

"How come?"

"Forget it." Charlie pulled a scrap piece of paper from his pocket with the name "Simone" and a seven-digit number scrawled in pencil underneath. "Got a quarter, Jim?"

I put a quarter in Charlie's hand. He popped the quarter into the slot, punched out the number, and stuck a finger up his nose while he waited for somebody to pick up on the other end. Then, with his finger still up his nose, he said, "Simone? ... Who you think? ... Guess ... Nope ... Nope ... Nope ... Wrong again ... Once more ... Nope ... It's Charlie ... You didn't think I was gonna call, eh? ... Don't lie ... What you doing? ... Yes, right now ... So come meet me ... What, you don't want to see me? ... Sneak out then ... Don't worry ... Anywhere ... I'm just with my buddy right now, but he's ... In how long? ... I won't be ... Don't worry ..."

The next day, when I got home from school, the phone was ringing. I picked it up in the kitchen. "Hello?"

"One of my ballerinas. He broke one of them."

"What?"

Charlie, his mother believed, had smashed one of the miniature pastel-coloured porcelain ballerina dancers she had received a few years back as a collective Christmas present from the staff at the Winners on Spadina Avenue, just north of King Street, where she'd been working full-time for the past six years.

There were three of them — one curtseying, one midway through a twirl, one balancing on tiptoe — and she'd placed them side by side on the sky-blue windowsill in her kitchen, facing indoors. When she came home from work that afternoon, the curtseying ballerina was scattered in pieces all over the kitchen floor.

"How come he'd do that?" I asked.

"You know his grandparents won't even speak to him?"

"What?"

"Or me."

"Oh."

"My father was a priest."

"Oh."

"Anglican," she said. "An Anglican priest."

"Oh."

"I grew up in Cornwall."

"Oh."

"And Charles never met him. My brothers, either. I have two brothers, and he's never met one of them. He thinks I was an only child."

"Oh."

"It's my fault."

"What?"

"His ... he didn't come home last night, you know?"

"Charlie?"

"But he must have come back during the day and then left again, because the ballerina, I know he ... he just needs a job."

"What?"

"Charles ... he'll be fine if he gets a job, don't you think?"

"Yes."

"I do. I think so."

"Oh."

"If you see him, just have him give me a call, Jim."

"Yes."

"Thank you, Jim. Sorry."

"Got a job for you" was the first thing Lucio said when the three of us met up at our regular picnic bench in Kingston Park two days later.

"What," Charlie asked, "there's an opening at the toy store?"

Lucio shook his head. "Nah, bro. Finished with that place. Place is gay. For some reason the manager — this Paki — got the idea I was stealing merchandise. He thinks I'm a thief. It's cause I'm Portuguese. They're racists at that store."

"Poor baby."

"I'm telling you. But don't even worry. I got this next job quick-fast. And no joke, it's the perfect job for you, Charlie. And you don't need no experience or nothing. Not even a résumé. Swear to God. And you could get paid in cash. It's perfect — the perfect job for you, boss."

"What is it?"

"This call centre," Lucio said. "Telemarketing. You sell vacations over the phone. It's easy. You sell them to old people. Twenty bucks commission every vacation you sell. No joke. I'll take you in tomorrow. Could make 'nuff cash."

"'Nuff?"

"I'm telling you."

"What kind of people work at the place?" Charlie asked.

"No joke, some strange people work there."

"Like who?"

"This one guy working next to me yesterday — the biggest prick I ever met. No joke. Guy's working next to me, so I keep trying to talk to him. Make some friendly chit-chat — I don't want to be a jerk or nothing — but every time I try and say something, guy moves away from me. Like I got chicken pox. No joke. He's the one who looks like he got diseases. Long hair, a beard. Some hippie or something. Rips in his jeans. Looks like he doesn't know how to shower. And in between calls he's reading this book. Got this painting of a naked broad on the cover, and I swear on my brother's turbo engine, she had the biggest bush I ever saw. I swear. No joke. And the guy, this hippie, he's reading it in between calls. It's not a porno or nothing. There's no pictures except for the cover. So I ask him what it's about, what the book's about. And he tells me I wouldn't understand. Calls me a Philistine." Lucio shook his head, frowning. "Guy thinks he's so smart, but he can't even talk right. He thinks I'm from Palestine?"

"Lucio, I don't think that's what —"

"I'm Portuguese, bro! Guy thinks I'm an Arab? I look like an Arab to you, Charlie?"

"No, Lucio."

"So then what's he so stupid for?"

"Guess he's just an idiot, Lucio."

"Guy's a dunce times ten, I'm telling you!"

Lucio then told us he had to cut our visit short because he had an appointment to buy fifty fake tokens from his buddy Mark, which he was planning to sell for double the price — sixty bucks — to this kid he knew named Sheldon.

"That's thirty bones right there," he said as he got up from the picnic bench.

As we watched him exit the park with his graceful, elastic stride, Charlie told me for the eleventh time in the past two days since he had allegedly spent the night at Simone's house, what the inside of her vagina looked like. And what the outside of her vagina looked like. And what looked different about the inside and the outside of her vagina compared to the inside and the outside of other vaginas he'd seen in the past. Then he asked me if I might like to do something with him, Simone, and one of Simone's friends later that evening. There was a good chance, if I came along, that I'd get to see the outside and maybe even the inside of Simone's friend's vagina.

"Can't," I said.

"Why not?"

"Gotta see my sister. She gets back today from her trip."

"You're gonna spend the night with her?"

"No."

"Then come after. What else you gonna do?"

"Dunno."

"Then I'll meet you at nine o clock. Back here."

"Fine."

"Scared?"

"No."

"I am *not* taking my shorts off."

"But you look so much better without them, Amanda."

"I do *not*, Erick."

"I love you."

"You do *not*."

"Do so."

"Erick, my dad's asleep upstairs, and my brother could —"

"Why does he go to bed so early?"

"Dad?"

"Yes."

"Because he wakes up early."

"What time?"

"Five o'clock."

"What does he do at five o'clock in the morning?"

"I don't know. Mopes around. Listens to Chopin."

"Then what does he do?"

"I don't know. Cleans. Naps. Brahms. He spends a lot of time cleaning. Look at this place. It's spotless. I hate it."

"Doesn't he work?"

"I told you fifty times, Erick. He's seventy-three years old."

"So?"

"So he's too old to work! And my mother was fairly well off. He inherited some money from her."

"How much?"

"Enough so that he can sit around and clean and listen to — *Erick!* Hands to yourself."

"You're like an orchid, you know that?"

"I am *not.*"

"Are so."

"*Not.*"

"*So.*"

"I hate this kitchen."

"It's not so bad."

"It's awful."

"It's just a regular kitchen."

"That's the problem. It's so … *North American.* So pragmatic. No character. This whole house. Everything's so … cold. Don't you think? Can't you just feel it? It's awful to be back. I wish I could die. I want to take my master's somewhere in Spain. If I don't, I'll die."

"What about your bedroom?"

"What about it?"

"I bet it's not so cold in your bedroom."

"Is that all you ever think about?"

"When I'm with you, yes."

"You disgust me."

"I do not."

"Do so."

"Sometimes I look at your thighs, Amanda, your creamy thighs, and I can't restrain —"

"Hands off, kiddo."

"Never."

"And my thighs aren't creamy. They're pasty. Pasty and plain. I don't know what you're talking about."

"They're like marble."

"They are *not*."

"Are so."

"Not."

"Venus thighs, you have."

"I do *not*. And this is *not* gonna work, Erick. You are *not* gonna charm my clothes off. *Not* happening. We just got off the plane, for heaven's sake. I haven't even seen my —"

"I'll carry you up to your bedroom. Let me carry you to your bedroom."

"You couldn't lift me if you tried."

"You wanna bet?"

"And I told you — my dad's asleep upstairs. And I do *not* want to wake him up. He needs his sleep."

"We'll be quiet."

Giggling: "Erick, you know how hard it is for me to stay quiet when we — stop it! Hands off."

"I won't tell anybody."

"Erick, what if my brother —"

"Remember that park in Rome, in broad daylight, and those two old men were sitting on the bench right in front of —"

"Yes."

"You were a wild woman. Fearless."

"But that was Rome."

"So?"

"This is home! And my seventy-five-year-old father is asleep one floor above us, and he needs his sleep, and I'm expecting my little brother to walk in any moment and —"

"I want to lick every inch of your body."

"Oh, I wish we didn't have to come back so *soon*."

"*Every inch!*"

"I hate Toronto."

"No skin shall go lickless!"

"I hate this kitchen."

"I love you, Amanda."

"I miss Madrid."

"I love the way you taste."

"Tapas are the greatest thing in the world, aren't they? I could live off tapas."

"I'm gonna eat you like a tapa."

"Erick, that tickles. Please. Stand up. Why don't you just wait one hour until there's no chance of my brother walking in? You can stay the night. We'll go down into my basement and —"

"Gobble, gobble, gobble."

"I am not taking them off, Erick."

"Yes, you are, my darling, or I'll rip them off with my chimera fangs and —"

"Erick, stop!"

"Not before I've had a taste of the most exquisite and delicious tapa known to man, which, of course, as we all know, can only be found between the thighs of —"

"Jim!"

"Who's Jim?"

"Oh, my goodness! How long have you been standing there?"

"Just got in now," I said.

"You're like a ghost. I didn't even hear you come in."

"Oh."

My sister quickly untangled herself from the lanky, freckle-faced young man who was kneeling in front of her and zipped up the fly on her khaki shorts. One of the straps on her loose green tank top was hanging down her arm, and she yanked it back over her shoulder, checked her fly again to make sure it was fully zipped, then, hopping over the two large dusty Mountain Equipment Co-op knapsacks resting on the kitchen floor in

front of her, ran to the doorway where I was standing to give
me a hug. We were now the same height (close to five foot two),
and her very large and heavy breasts (she wasn't wearing a bra)
pressed into my chest, not my face, as we embraced.

"Oh, my God, it's *soooo* weird to be back, Jim," she said as she
let go of my body.

"Yeah?"

"Oh, my God!" Then, speaking rapidly, as if her voice were
on fast-forward, she told me she had *soooo* much to tell me that
she didn't even know where to begin telling me all the things
she had to tell me because there was *sooooo* much to tell me.
Really, she had a million things to tell me, but right now she was
jet-lagged as hell and discombobulated, and travelling was *soooo*
hectic and it was *sooooooo* weird to think that just seven hours ago
she'd been in Heathrow Airport. *Seven hours ago she was in the
United Kingdom* — and now she was back in Toronto and that
was *sooooooo* awful and she had *sooooooooo* much to tell me and if I
never got a chance to go to Europe I would die.

"Oh."

"How's Dad been?" she asked.

"He's —"

"Oh, I forgot." Amanda pointed an outspread palm to the
blushing fellow who had gotten up from his knees and was now
standing behind her in the kitchen. "This is my friend, Erick."

Erick — he had the biggest Adam's apple I'd ever seen and
was wearing a grey University of Toronto T-shirt, frayed jean
shorts, and Teva sandals — forced a smile. "She's told me lots
about you. How's it going?"

"Fine."

"It's the weirdest thing," my sister said. "I met him at this
hostel in Barcelona. Barcelona, by the way, is the greatest place
in the world, Jim, absolutely the most fantastic place. Gaudí's

architecture — oh, my God, the greatest thing, *soooo* whimsical — and the hostel we were staying in was really cheap, only four-teen euros a night. And that's really good for Barcelona. Most places are, like, twenty euros a night, seriously, and this place was right downtown, right by the Ramblas."

"The Ramblas?"

"It's the greatest thing."

"Oh."

"And Erick —" my sister turned to him, and he reddened "— was staying there, too, at the hostel, I mean."

"Oh."

"And it turns out he's also from Toronto. He lives in the east end."

"Oh."

"It's such a small world, Jim. Really. And you only realize it once you travel. Once you see how connected everybody is."

"Yeah?"

"It's true. But here's the craziest thing."

"What?"

"We both had tickets for the same flight back to Toronto. Me and Erick. Both leaving from Heathrow, same day, time, everything." Amanda shook her head. "Fate. Must be. Has to be fate. I mean, how else can you —"

"Destiny," Erick interjected, stepping forward. "I prefer the word *destiny*. It's less ... *fatalistic*. You know? Less about the inevitable."

My sister squinted, scratched her chin. "He studies philoso-phy at U of T."

"Oh."

"And classics," Erick added. "I also study classics."

"Oh."

"He's very smart," Amanda said.

"Am not."

"Are so."

"Not."

"He is," my sister said. Then she stared at me for a few moments as if I'd just asked her out on a date and she was thinking of a way to let me down kindly. Her face seemed somehow wider and longer than before her trip.

"Which was the favourite place you —" But before I could finish the question my sister flung her head backward and let out a loud and sorrowful "*Uggh*, it's *soooo* weird to be home." As she did this, because of the speed and jerkiness of her movement — and her lack of a bra and the largeness of her breasts — out poked the tip of her left tit from her loose green tank top.

She didn't notice.

It was just hanging there.

Her big, fleshy saucer nipple was just hanging there.

"I can't believe it," she said, making a face as if she was about to cry. "God, I feel like I'm about to cry. Really. I can't actually believe I'm *really* here in this house. *Really*. Back *here*. It's so awful. Look at this place. It's … what are you staring at, Jim?"

I glanced up. "What?"

She looked where I'd been looking. "Oh, my goodness."

And before she had time to shove her breast back into her shirt, I was already halfway out the front door on my way to Kingston Park to meet Charlie.

A skinny girl with a long neck and short orange hair who looked very much like a teenage Jamie Lee Curtis came to a halt in front of our picnic bench. She was wearing a tight yellow T-shirt with ATTITUDE printed in sparkly silver lettering over the chest and a white tennis skirt. Simone's friend — dumpy with skin

the colour of an almond and a chubby-cheeked, chipmunkish
face — was hovering a little way back, talking on her cellphone.

"What's up, Simone?" Charlie said to the orange-haired girl.

She rolled her eyes. "I don't know. This smelly guy followed
us halfway here. He was nasty, Charlie. Such a creep."

"He try anything?"

"No, but he smelled like piss and he kept on walking right
up behind us. It was nasty."

"But he didn't try nothing?"

"No."

"I *thought* he was gonna try something." Simone's friend
clicked her cellphone shut, stepped forward. "Like, come try
and talk to us or something, or try and take us somewhere, like,
into an alleyway or up into some dirty apartment or something.
Then he just turned the corner and went down another street.
But not before he followed us for so long."

"He was a creep," said Simone.

"There's so many creeps around," her friend said.

"I know," said Simone.

"Two weeks ago," said her friend, "this guy was looking at
me on the subway, smiling at me, and I didn't even notice for
a little while, but then I looked down at his pants and his dick
was hanging out. Just like that. Nobody noticed except me. And
then he went down to touch it, but I shouted for everybody in
the subway to look. 'This guy's a pervert! Right here! Everybody
look, this guy's a pervert! His dick's out!' And he couldn't even
get it back in his pants quick enough, so everybody saw what
he was doing. I think he got arrested or something. I'm not
afraid to scream when that stuff happens, you know. I'm not just
gonna say nothing."

"I would've laughed at him if he tried that," Simone said.

"No, you wouldn't," said her friend.

"It would be funny."

"It's not funny," said her friend.

"I'm not scared of his dick on a subway full of people," Simone said. "He's not gonna rape me."

"Whatever," her friend said.

"You girls are so rude," Charlie said. "I don't believe it. You're not even gonna introduce yourselves to my buddy?"

They both giggled.

"I'm Simone," the taller one said.

"Fatima," said the other.

"Jim," I said.

"Hi, Jim," said Fatima.

"Hello."

"What's up, Jim?" Simone asked.

"Hello," I said again.

"Got something on your shirt," Charlie said, pointing at Simone's chest. When she looked down, he flicked her nose with his finger.

"You're such an asshole," Simone said, punching Charlie in the arm.

"This girl thinks she's tough," Charlie said.

"I am tough."

"Okay, tough guy," Charlie said.

"Shut up."

Charlie grinned at her. "You ever been to this park before?"

"No."

"How about I give you a tour then?"

Simone nibbled on her baby-blue pinky fingernail. "Let's go."

Kingston Park was flat and square and consisted of a basketball court, a small playground, a public bathroom, twenty-four large trees (I'd counted), some bushes, a soccer net, a number of picnic benches and regular benches, and lots of grass. The picnic bench where I was sitting — our regular picnic bench — was next to the basketball court, and Charlie had engraved MR. GLICKMAN IS A QUEER, MR. GLICKMAN SUCKS COCK, MR. GLICKMAN SUCKS MR. PERCHES' COCK, MR. GLICKMAN SUCKS MR. PERCHES' COCK WHILE MR. PERCHES SHOVES A RUGBY BALL UP MRS. WORSNOP'S ASS, MR. GLICKMAN SUCKS MRS. WORSNOP'S COCK, and MRS. WORSNOP HAS A COCK into the wooden surface with his house key. WU-TANG FOREVER, I HATE CONDOMS, and PORTUGUESE 4 LIFE had also been engraved, but by unknown sources.

As Fatima sat beside me, we watched Charlie and Simone stroll toward the playground.

Fatima looked at her shoes — white Nike cross-trainers with pink soles. She wiped some dirt off the side of one of them with two fingers. "That's the problem with white shoes. It's so annoying. You can't ever wear them anywhere without getting them all dirty. If you wanna keep them looking nice, you always have to be cleaning them. *Always.*" She peered at my black Adidas low-tops. "See?"

"What?"

"You don't have to worry about walking in mud or anything like that. Your shoes, they look clean one way or the other. You're lucky. But my shoes, every time I walk through a park, or if I walk in a puddle or in mud or anything like that, they get all dirty, and I have to clean them. I'm always cleaning them."

"Maybe you should get black shoes then?"

Fatima glanced up at me. "What? No. I like *white* shoes."

"Oh."

"It's Jim, right? Your name's Jim?"

"Yes."

"That short for anything?"

"Not really."

"So you mean your parents just named you Jim and that's it?"

"No."

"So it *is* short for something?"

"I guess. Yeah."

"What?"

"What, what?"

"What's it short for? What's Jim short for?"

"Oh, James. Jim's short for James. But nobody calls me that."

"How come?"

"Dunno."

"Which one you like better — James or Jim?"

"Probably Jim."

"How come?"

"Dunno. 'Cause I'm used to it, probably."

"I like James more," said Fatima.

"Oh."

"Know why?"

"No."

"'Cause I knew this guy named Jim, and he was a big asshole."

"Oh."

"I hate him. I hope he gets hit by a car or something. Such a jerk. He was such a jerk. Know what he said to me?"

"No."

"Called me a dyke. That's what he called me, 'cause I wouldn't have sex with him. Sorry, but I'm not just gonna have sex with anybody, and that doesn't make me a dyke. Don't think so. Some girls will do it with anybody they meet. They don't even care. If you ask them to, they'll do it. But at most, when I first meet a guy, I'll give him a hand job. That's as far as I go. Sorry."

"Oh."

"And I won't give a guy head until I've met him at least three times. Some girls go around giving everybody head. That's not me. I'm not like that. I have rules. I'm not some slut like that."

"Oh."

"And you know what he told my friend?"

"Who?"

"Jim."

"Jim?"

"This guy," said Fatima. "The guy who called me a dyke."

"Oh."

"He told my friend that I told him I wanted to give her head and then she thought the reason why I don't go around giving guys head like most other girls is 'cause I only give girls head and that I'm a dyke."

"Oh."

"I don't go around giving guys head 'cause I'm not a slut like that. It's not 'cause I'm some dyke. I'm not even bisexual like some girls."

"Oh."

"But I've only ever given head to four guys, and one of them was my boyfriend for seven and a half months so that doesn't really count. Or maybe it counts, but in a different way. I mean, I didn't do it 'cause I was a slut or nothing like that."

"Oh."

"And that's not a lot of guys compared to most girls."

"Oh."

"But I hate that guy Jim so much. I hope he gets in a plane crash or something. If all of a sudden a brick fell from the sky and hit him in the head and he died on the spot, I wouldn't even care. It's too bad you have the same name as him."

"Oh."

"But so your parents don't even ever call you James?"

"No."

"If I were your parents, I'd always call you James."

"Oh."

"Jim sounds too much like bum."

"Bum?"

"Yeah, bum."

"Jim doesn't sound like bum."

"Sure it does," she said. "Jim. Bum. Jim. Bum. Jim. Bum. They sound alike, see?"

"No."

"Jim. Bum. Jim. Bum. They do. I would never name my kid Jim."

"Because it sounds too much like bum?"

"No. Because that guy, that asshole. I wouldn't want my kid to remind me of him."

"Oh."

"But I know a kid named James, too."

"Oh."

"Kind of looks like a psycho or something."

"Yeah?"

"Yeah. It's 'cause he has all these pimples on his chin and he's always twitching his head around. He's in my math class. I think he's a psycho."

"You think?"

"Yeah, probably. I don't know. He probably has a lot of pet snakes or something. He looks like one of those kids who have a lot of pet snakes."

"Oh."

"I would never fool around with a kid like that."

"Oh."

"I wouldn't even give him a hand job. Wouldn't wanna touch that."

"Oh."

"And I wouldn't name my kid James, either. But not 'cause of him."

"Oh."

"'Cause I don't really like that name. Just in general. When I say it, it reminds me of a mushy apple. You know when you think an apple's gonna be really good and crunchy and you take a bite out of it and then it's actually mushy?"

"Yes."

"That's what I think of when I say the name James. And plus — I already know what I'm gonna name my kids. If I had a boy, I'd name him Duane. And if I had a girl, I'd name her Alicia. *Those* are nice names. What would you name your kids?"

"My kids?"

"Yeah. What would you name them?"

"Dunno."

"How about Bradley?"

"Maybe."

"I like the name Bradley. If I were you, I'd name my kid Bradley."

"Why not Duane?"

"Because a kid named Duane wouldn't suit being your kid."

"Oh."

"A kid named Bradley would suit you much better. Your parents should have named you Bradley."

"Then what would I name my kid?"

"You could name him Malcolm."

"Oh."

"My ex-boyfriend's name is Malcolm. He's the only guy I've ever had sex with."

"What?"

"I went out with him for seven and a half months, too. I'm not just gonna have sex with anybody."

"Oh."

"Whatever." Fatima looked at my shoes again. "Where did you buy your shoes?"

"Dunno. Foot Locker, I think."

"You think those shoes would look good on a girl?"

"Maybe."

"Do they come in white?"

"Dunno."

"They're nice shoes."

"Yours are pretty nice, too," I said.

"No, they're not."

"Oh."

Then, after silently studying each other's shoes for what must have been more than two minutes, Fatima said, "I don't think they're coming back."

They weren't coming back. Fatima called Simone on her cell, and Simone told her that she and Charlie had left the park and that they were just walking around. They might go to her house. Maybe to Charlie's. Simone might just go home on her own. They didn't know what they were going to do. But they weren't coming back to the park.

"She always does this," Fatima huffed, putting her cell back into her handbag. "She's always ditching me like that."

"Oh."

"She's a slut, too. Know how many guys she's given head to?"

"No."

"Seventeen. And she's never had a serious boyfriend or nothing like that. Once, at this party, she gave head to two guys in the same night. She's a slut like that. I don't even know why she's my friend."

"You don't like her?"

Fatima glared at me. "I never said I didn't *like* her."

"Oh."

"Why would I chill with her if I didn't *like* her? You think I'm gonna chill with somebody who I don't even *like*?"

"No. It's just that you said —"

"You think I'm some kind of slut or something who doesn't even have her own mind and just chills with somebody because she's cool or something? Sorry. I'm not like that. That is *not* me. What I said is sometimes I don't know why she's my friend. That doesn't mean I don't *like* her."

"Oh."

"What's wrong with you, anyway?"

"What?"

"You can't even talk or something."

"What?"

"You're stupid, eh?"

"No."

"Whatever, you stupid Jim-Bum idiot." Fatima got up from the picnic bench and began stomping out of the park the same way she had come. I could hear her punching in a number on her cellphone as she left.

I knew it was Charlie's mother, but I picked the phone up, anyway, mostly because my house was so quiet, which made the ringing sound like a loud and urgent alarm. "Hello?"

There was a long pause before she said, "Hi, Jim. I know it's late. And I'm sure he's not with you. I'm sure Charles isn't with you."

"Oh."

"Is he with you?"

"No."

"Right. Like I thought. He's probably … I don't know. It doesn't matter. I'm sorry, Jim."

"It's okay."

"Thank you. You're so quiet, Jim, and you ... you understand ..."

I didn't say anything.

"You ... you're ... you know that when I was a lot younger I had a friend named Pat? Did you know that, Jim?"

"No."

"We were great friends, just like you and Charles. We went to high school together, spent all our time together. We were great friends."

"Oh."

"And later on, Jim, we moved to Toronto and rented an apartment together on Palmerston Avenue, a two-bedroom basement apartment in a beautiful old Victorian house on Palmerston Avenue. And you had to wear slippers everywhere inside so you wouldn't get splinters from the wooden floors."

"Oh."

"Does Charles have a girlfriend?"

"What?"

"A girlfriend. He's never brought a girl home to me. Not once. I mean, he must talk to girls at school, right?"

"I guess. I don't —"

"Well, *Pat* had a boyfriend. She was very beautiful and tall, and her boyfriend was much shorter than her and funny-looking. He had this way about him, this way of smiling, this — Do you smile at girls, Jim?"

"Me?"

"What about Charles? Does he smile at girls? Does he go around smiling at girls?"

"Smiling?"

"You know what, Jim?"

"What?"

"You're very friendly, Jim. You're a very friendly and gentle kid."

"Oh."

"We both worked at different restaurants."

"Who?" I asked.

"And Pat worked late at her restaurant, much later than me, and my hours were always getting jumbled all over the place because that's the way it was with my job. At the time there was no steady schedule. And one night I was all alone, and I heard his steps, his sneakers, and then suddenly he was just there in the kitchen. He just slid in. I mean, would you ever do that, just slide into somebody's house like that?"

"What?"

"Would you just drop in on somebody without even letting them know you were coming? Not even any sort of warning? No phone call or anything? Who does such a thing? Who does something like that? Who just walks into somebody's house uninvited? Who does that, Jim?"

"I don't know."

"Would you do that?"

"No."

"Would Charlie?"

"What?"

"I told him Pat was working and that she wouldn't be home till late and he should come back tomorrow when she wasn't working so that he could see her because right now she was at work and she wasn't here so he should come back tomorrow during the day when she *would* be here, but he just slid in, Jim. I couldn't ... Jim?"

"Yes."

"I didn't lead him on, Jim. I didn't want him."

"Who?"

"I remember his shoes ..."

"Oh."

"Those white sneakers. Brand-new sneakers, tennis shoes. I don't think he played tennis, but he was wearing these tennis shoes, and I remember how *new* they seemed. They were … *squeaky*, you know?"

"Squeaky?"

"They *squeaked*."

"Oh."

"When he walked."

"Oh."

"Forget it. Tennis is a stupid game, I think. I think it's stupid. Have you ever played?"

"Tennis?"

"Yes."

"No."

"You haven't?"

"No."

"I don't think Charlie has, either. I couldn't see him playing tennis. It's not his sort of game."

"Oh."

"And I don' think *he* had, either, but he was still wearing these squeaky brand-new white tennis shoes, and I tried to fight him, but he was too … he was too *quick*. And the next day he told Pat all sorts of things, that I was trying to unbuckle his belt with my teeth, that I was on my knees begging him. Pat believed him, every word he said, and he just smiled the way he did, the way he always did, and I knew what my father would think and what my brothers would think and what my mother would think. I knew how strict and stubborn they all were. But I didn't care, Jim. There was no question in my mind. The baby was … he was mine …"

Ricky Tantrum.

"This job Jeffrey got me is too easy, Jim," Charlie said on the second Saturday of summer vacation after beating me in a game of one-on-one at the Kingston Park courts. We were sitting across from each other at our regular picnic bench. "I'm a master, Jim. The king. I'm making tons of cash."

"Really?"

Charlie took off his Padres cap, scratched his hair, then put it back on. "It's the truth, Jim. All day. Over and over. 'Hello there, ma'am, are you ready for some good news?' 'Well, sure. Who is this?' 'This is Ricky Tantrum calling on behalf of Sun Beach Travel Agency. It's your lucky day, ma'am, because you — yes, *you* — thanks to Sun Beach Travel Agency have won an all-inclusive, all-paid, one-week vacation to Miami, Florida, for two! Pack your bathing suit, because you're heading south!' 'Oh, my gosh! Me?' 'That's right, you. You, ma'am. Everything has already been arranged and organized — and, of course, paid for. The only thing left for you to do is pack your bag. Oh, and don't forget your sunscreen, because, let me tell you, it's gonna be hot. And us folks down here at Sun Beach Travel Agency don't want you burning up out there on the beach.' 'Oh, gee, I've never won anything before in my life.' 'Well, ma'am, looks like your luck has taken a turn for the better, doesn't it? Now listen here. What I'm going to do is send one of my guys over to your place to drop off the tickets and give you all the details. His name is Edward Campbell, a real nice fellow — any questions you got, he'll be happy to answer them. But before I send Eddy over to get you all set up, what I gotta do is write down your credit-card number. There's a small tax on the cost of the trip — one hundred percent deductible, *of course* — that we're required to collect before —' 'Oh, of course, sir. Yes, yes. Let me just find my purse.'" Charlie bounced his Spalding indoor/outdoor basketball hard against the top of the picnic bench, then caught it with one hand. "*Boom!* Just like that. Another sale."

"Sale?" I said.

"Fine. A scam. *Sale*," he mimicked in a high-pitched, whiny voice. "These old idiots, Jim, they don't know what the hell's going on, anyway. I could call ninety percent of them back a few weeks later and convince them they'd actually just gotten back from the Caribbean. 'Hello there, ma'am, this is Ricky Tantrum calling from Sun Beach Travel Agency. I'm just checking up on you again to hear more about your trip.' 'My trip?' 'Yes, ma'am, your vacation in the Bahamas. You won tickets a month ago. You were there for a week.' 'The Bahamas?' 'Yes, ma'am, you stayed in a little thatched house by the beach. You told me there was a black man who wore a straw dress and served you pina coladas in coconut shells while you were tanning on the beach. You said you had a marvellous time.' 'Who are you?' 'I'm Ricky Tantrum from Sun Beach Travel Agency, ma'am. The fellow who brought you the good news that you won a vacation. That was a month ago. I called you last week when you got back to make sure you had a good time. You told me all about it. You said you had a blast. I'm just checking up on you again.' 'Oh, well, that's nice of you, Mr. Tantrum.' 'It's my pleasure, ma'am. But I've got to run. It's real busy in the office. Lots of paperwork to do.' 'Oh, of course.' 'You take care now, ma'am.' 'You, too, Mr. Tantrum.' And you see, Jim?"

"See what?"

"The old lady's left thinking she just got back from a beach house in the Bahamas. Who cares if she went on the trip or not? If she believes it — who cares? What's the problem?"

"Dunno. She never went."

"That's not the point."

"What?"

"Who cares what actually happened if you believe something else? It doesn't make a difference."

"It doesn't?"

"Forget it," Charlie said. "I gotta go, anyway."

"Where you going?"

"Gotta meet my dad."

"Your dad?"

"Yeah, he's taking me out to dinner at this restaurant downtown. A steak house."

"Really?"

Charlie got up from the picnic bench. "Yes, Jim, *really*."

"It's Saturday night, Jimmy," Nikolai said. "What are you doing sitting around here by yourself, eh? What are you thinking about all the time? How many ginger ales you drank today?"

"Dunno. Two, three —"

"Four, Jimmy." Nikolai stuck his index finger into the hairy inside of his right ear and twisted. "You drank four ginger ales since you been here."

"So?"

"So look at you, Jimmy! You look like … like …" He pulled his finger from his ear, inspected the pale yellow substance gathered on the tip. Then, frowning at the earwax as if it had disappointed him in some way, he flicked it onto the floor. "You look like a … like some octopus, Jimmy."

"An octopus?"

"Sure. Like some lonely octopus hiding at the bottom of the sea. You frown like some octopus."

"But octopuses don't have —"

"The octopus, Jimmy, they are the saddest animal. Maximum sadness. All of them. All the time."

"What?"

Nikolai wiggled a greasy finger at my nose. "Who likes an octopus? Who's gonna be friends with an octopus, Jimmy? Nobody. Kaput. Zero. All the fish, they run away from the octopus. The sharks, they eat the octopus. The dolphins, they don't like the octopus. And know why, Jimmy? Know why nobody likes the octopus?"

"No."

"Because the octopus, he thinks nobody likes him. So then nobody likes him. And then, because nobody likes him, because he thinks nobody likes him, he hides at the bottom of the sea. Under some rock. In the dark. Alone. All the time. Maximum sadness. Frowning all the —"

"Octopuses don't frown, Nick. They don't even have —"

"Sure they do, Jimmy! You ever seen an octopus? You ever see how much sadness is on his face?"

"I've seen an octopus."

"Well, then you ever see how he never likes to talk to nobody?"

"What?"

"You ever see how when you try to talk to the octopus he just frowns at you and goes back to his rock? You ever see how an octopus mopes around? It's just like you! You're an octopus, Jimmy!"

"I'm not an octopus."

"Then how come you sit around here so much all the time with that frown, Jimmy? How come you don't find yourself a woman, eh? Even Oleg, that fool, that stupid fool, he found some girl! A nice girl, too. What's her name? He brought her around here not so long from now. What was her name? Anna? April?"

"Angela."

"Yeah, Angel."

"*Angela.*"

"Angel, Angela, April, Ada, Anna, sure. Her face, it was nice. And some nice knockers to add. Not yet so big, but in a couple of years, I don't know, maybe … maybe they should grow some more. Who knows? Some, Jimmy, they never stop growing, you know that?"

"What?"

"The knockers. On a woman. Like noses … they're like noses, Jimmy. Noses and knockers. They don't stop growing! Never. Bigger and bigger they grow! All the time! And who knows, maybe when — Angel, that's her name?"

"Angela."

"Sure, when Angel reaches my age, when she's an old woman, hey, maybe her knockers, they will be like beach balls, eh? Beach balls, Jimmy!" Nikolai clapped his hands together, delighted at the prospect. "Beach balls! Ha, ha! You like beach balls, Jimmy?"

"Sure."

"That's right, Jimmy! That's why I like you, Jimmy! But you see …" Nikolai licked a breadcrumb from his moustache, leaned closer to me. "You see, Jimmy, with them, with my nephew and his Angel, still it is something fresh for them. Something new. Still there is some … some passion. They still have passion, you know?"

"Passion?"

"Sure. That means they are still … mysteries. To each other they are still mysteries. That's what brings passion."

"What?"

"Mysteries. Things you don't know, Jimmy. Secrets. That means passion."

"Oh."

"You don't know nothing, Jimmy."

"Oh."

"And smartie pants, your friend, Farley, he has a girl, too, no?"

"Yes."

"Okay, sure. Him, he's not so stupid. He understands how he can get something. Some good stuff. He knows some things. But if Oleg, that fool — *that fool who has to spend his summer also in school because he is too much of a turkey to pass any of his courses* — if he can find some woman with some okay knockers like that, you could do the same, Jimmy. All you need is to put on a fancy shirt sometime. Silk maybe. A nice collar. Fancy, Jimmy. A woman likes it when a man is fancy. If he has a silver buckle on his shoes, they like that. A woman sees a silver buckle, and know what she thinks?"

"What?"

"She sees a silver buckle and she thinks, *That's somebody who could buy me something nice. That's somebody who could get me some fancy jewellery or maybe some good cutlery.* And then know what she thinks?"

"What?"

"She thinks — and this is what's important, Jimmy — she thinks, *That's somebody who I maybe will give the good stuff to because he could buy me some nice perfume or maybe some good cutlery or some fancy jewellery. She thinks, That's somebody who maybe I will even give him some ... some special good stuff. Something extra. A tune-up maybe.*"

"A tune-up?"

"You know, your back bucket, Jimmy?"

"What?"

"Where you sit, you know? Your dump truck. She uses her, ha, you know, her mouth. She uses her mouth on it. Your back bucket. Your dump truck."

"You mean she —"

"Jimmy?"

"Yes?"

Nikolai grabbed my arm, pulled my face close to his. "You want to turn into a piece of furniture who just sits in some place and gets dusty and never leaves for his whole life?"

"No."

"You don't want to be some chair or a table who never goes nowhere?"

"No."

"You want to get some good stuff sometime?"

"Sure."

"You do?"

"Yeah."

"So then stop being an octopus and get out of here!" Nikolai hollered into my ear. Then he let go of my arm and gave me a wink that made half his face, like paper, crinkle into a knot of wrinkles.

My father was waiting for me on our porch steps when I got home. "I have good news, Jim."

I sat next to him.

"I received a phone call today. We've won a vacation to Fiji for three weeks."

"Fiji?"

"Yes, Jim, Fiji. You, your sister, and me. We leave in four days. The man from the travel agency, this Ricky Tantrum, he should be here any minute to drop the tickets off."

"Ricky Tantrum?"

"Yes. That was his name."

"Oh."

"This is good, Jim."

"Oh."

"I'm ready to do something like this. Go somewhere. Leave for a little while."

"Oh."

"I can't keep on like this. It's … I have to let things finish."

"Oh."

"You've only known me in mourning, Jim."

"Oh."

"This phone call was a blessing."

"Oh."

My father, like Fatima had a few weeks before, looked at my shoes. After a little while, he said, "You know, your mother, she was … she was nothing like you are, Jim. She was very loud. Talked a lot."

"Oh."

"You don't … you don't talk a lot."

"I know."

"I'm looking forward to this, Jim. I'm looking forward to this trip."

"You are?"

"Yes, Jim."

I glanced at his shoes, worn-out Hush Puppies. "Me, too," I finally said. Then we sat there, my father and me, staring at each other's shoes and waiting for Ricky Tantrum to show up.

Acknowledgements

Most importantly, I would like to thank Morris Wolfe; his encouragement and feedback have kept me afloat. I would also like to thank my late grandmother, Edith Lowbeer, who graciously put me up while the bulk of this book was written.

More Great Fiction from Dundurn

Something Remains
by Hassan Ghedi Santur
978-1-55488-465-0
$21.99

Andrew Christiansen, a war photographer turned cab driver, is having a bad year. His mother has just died; his father, on the verge of a nervous breakdown, gets arrested; and he's married to a woman he doesn't love. Keeping Andrew sane is his beloved camera through which he captures the many Torontonians who ride in his taxi. *Something Remains* probes the various ways humans grieve when the lives they build for themselves fall apart. And it speaks of the joy we find in what remains.

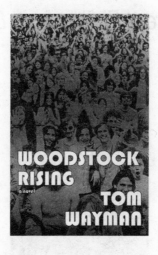

Woodstock Rising
by Tom Wayman
978-1-55002-860-7
$21.99

In this extraordinary black comedy shot full of the social and political issues of 1969–70, a group of college students sets out to put a satellite into orbit in homage to the recent Woodstock Festival. Accompanied by a young Canadian graduate student, the activists break into a mothballed missile silo and have big plans for their loot, including a nuclear warhead, which might culminate in the Light Show to End All Light Shows over the Nevada desert.

Valley of Fire
by Steven Manners
978-1-55488-406-3
$21.99

John Munin is a rational man, a gifted psychiatrist who believes that the soul and psyche are interesting only in dissection. More susceptible to Munin's searching analysis, though, is Penelope, who suffers from obsessive-compulsive disorder and is Munin's star patient. Munin plans to present Penelope's case at a major medical conference in Las Vegas. But tragedy strikes on the eve of the event, and the probing psychiatrist's orderly world crumbles in the crucible of the Valley of Fire.

Available at your favourite bookseller.

DUNDURN PRESS
www.dundurn.com

What did you think of this book?

Visit www.dundurn.com for
reviews, videos, updates, and more!